ROY CLINTON

NATIONAL BESTSELLING AUTHOR

CANDY MAN

A MIDNIGHT MARAUDER ADVENTURE

CANDY MAN

A Midnight Marauder Adventure

Roy Clinton

Published by Top Westerns Publishing (www.TopWesterns.com), 3730 Kirby Dr., Suite 1130, Houston, TX 77098. Contact info@TopWesterns.com for more information.

Book Design by Teresa Lauer: Info@TeresaLauer.com.

Cover by Laurie Barboza: DesignStashBooks@gmail.com

Copy Editor: Sharon Smith

Substantive Editor: Maxwell Morelli

Other Books by Roy Clinton

Lost
Midnight Marauder
Return of Midnight Marauder
Revenge of Midnight Marauder
Midnight Marauder and the President of the United States
Love Child
Bad to the Bone
Purgatory Creek
(To be released in 2020)

These books and others can be found on
www.TopWesterns.com and *www.Amazon.com*.

Audio versions of these books can be found on
www.Audible.com as well as on iTunes and Apple Books.

**Dedicated to
Montgomery Escue
A Real Man Who is
Outstanding in Every Way**

Table of Contents

PROLOGUE

1874

Wednesday, June 24th
Brooklyn Heights, New York

The saloon was dark and stank of stale beer. Bill Mosher sat on a stool, as per his instructions, and waited. It was the middle of the morning. The only people in a saloon this hour either had no other place they needed to be or they were booze hounds who couldn't hold a job.

"What are you having?" The bartender seemed bored with his job and not the least bit interested in what Bill wanted. To him, Bill was just another interruption in his day. Another customer who would make demands on his time, drink a few beers, make a mess, and then leave without so much as a "thank you" or a tip.

"Beer." As Bill ordered his drink, he slowly looked around the saloon, wondering who he was meeting. There were a few patrons but no one who was paying any attention to him. At the far end of the bar, Bill spotted someone he thought might be his contact. He waited but the man never looked his way.

He thought back to the letter he received and wondered how anyone had selected him. Reaching in his pocket, he retrieved the letter that he found on the deck of his boat. Someone had left it near the gangplank, weighted with a rock.

I have a special job that fits your skills. Outstanding pay. A big cent. Meet me on Wednesday, June 24th at 10:00 a.m. in the saloon at 62 Montague Street between Pierrepont Place and Hicks Street. Tell no one. Sit at the bar and wait. I'll contact you.

Bill fingered the letter and wondered who sent it. When it talked about big money, he wondered how much that really meant. And what did he mean about a "big cent?" He refolded the letter and placed it back in his pocket and took a sip of his beer. Bill had never really acquired a taste for beer but he wanted to fit in. Ordering anything else would have made him stand out.

Fifteen minutes passed and still no one showed the slightest interest in him. No new customers had entered since he arrived. Bill wondered if he had the wrong day. Once again, he removed the letter from his pocket and verified the date for the meeting.

From the back corner of the saloon, a man approached the

bartender and ordered another beer. As he was taking it back to his table, he made eye contact with Bill and gave the smallest indication with his head he should follow. Bill picked up his beer and followed the stranger.

The stranger took a long swallow of his beer and set it back on the table. Bill noticed the man was wearing expensive clothes. He wore a beautifully tailored suit and had a beaver top hat and an ivory inlaid cane on the table. The stranger's shirt looked to be made of silk as did his black tie.

He looked at Bill as though he were trying to see into his soul. Bill was self-conscious about his appearance, knowing he was not a handsome man and his clothes were well-worn and dirty.

As Bill watched, the stranger withdrew his wallet from the inside pocket of his suit coat. He withdrew 10 one hundred-dollar bills and slid them across the table. Bill's eyes grew large and he could feel his heart race as he eyed the money. While he had seen hundred-dollar bills before, he had never seen ten of them, much less thought he would ever be able to call them his own.

"What's that for? What do I have to do?"

The stranger furtively looked from side to side. Confident they were not being overheard, the stranger laid out his plan.

"That's expense money. There is a child you're going to snatch. The family will give you twenty thousand dollars to get him back. Half the money will be mine and the other half will be yours. Do you have any problem with taking a child?"

Bill didn't hesitate. "None whatsoever. But I don't see why I'll need to spend any of this money on expenses. I can just snatch the child and wait for his parents to pay."

"This is not going to be so simple of a job. First, the child is in Philadelphia. And secondly, you're going to need help. I want you to find some men to help you. However, you can never mention me. They're not to even know I exist. So far as they're concerned, the kidnapping is all your idea.

"You're not to get in a hurry. Careful planning will make this the perfect crime. No one has ever done this before. You'll be the first. Do you think you can do that?"

Bill's mouth slowly turned to a smile. "Of course, I can. And I'm a real good planner. Where do I find this child?"

"You and your accomplices are to go to this address in Philadelphia." The stranger slid a piece of paper across to Bill. "The boy's name is Charles Brewster Ross and he's four years old. They call him Charley. His father is Christian Ross. On Friday, June 26th, Mr. Ross is sending his ailing wife and three of his children on summer vacation to Atlantic City. That'll just leave Charley, Walter, and the baby at home with their father. As soon after that as possible, I want you to take Charley and then get someone to care for him in a secret location."

Bill listened and took in all he was being told. "Here's a map to a cave about thirty miles north of Philadelphia. I have already stocked it with food, blankets, and other supplies. There's a little stream right beside it so you'll have plenty of water. It's in the middle of nowhere. Your man can keep Charley safe there for as long as necessary."

"How will we ever be able to keep him quiet while taking him to the cave? He's likely to be screaming his lungs out."

The stranger smiled and pulled a brown bottle from his coat and set it on the table. "This is chloroform. You put a little bit on a cloth and have him breathe it and he'll be out in an instant. Just don't use too much and don't use it more than necessary."

Mosher pulled the stopper from the bottle and sniffed it. "It smells sweet."

"Don't do that, fool. One more breath and you won't smell anything because you'll be out cold." Mosher put the cork back and refolded the map and then put both items in his pockets.

The stranger looked intently at Mosher. "This is important. The boy is not to be harmed in any way. If he's harmed, you'll answer to me. And you don't want to see what I do when I get angry."

Bill nodded his head in agreement. His eyes moved back and forth as he formulated a plan. "I think I want two, maybe three men to help me. I see how they can help me get the lay of the land. And it'll probably take two men to get him to the cave and take care of him."

"Now you see why you need expense money. You'll need to get to Philadelphia and you'll need to have money for food and lodging while you plan your job and then while we're waiting for Mr. Ross to pay."

Bill looked intently at the stranger. "I don't even know your name."

"No, you don't. And you're not going to. All you need from me is the address of the child and money for expenses. After you take the child, you're to write a letter to Mr. Ross—disguise it as best you can—and demand twenty thousand dollars for the return of Charley."

"How am I supposed to contact you?"

"You'll not need to contact me. I'll know what you're doing. I'll know when you take the boy and when you've been paid for his return. When you get the money, I'll let you know where we're to meet."

Bill took a swallow of his beer and made a face as he tasted its bitterness. "When do I get started?"

The stranger stood, picked up his cane, placed his hat on his head and said, "Now." Bill watched as the stranger walked out of the saloon, then he smiled as he picked up the stack of bills on the table. For the first time in his life, he felt rich.

CHAPTER 1

Saturday, July 4th
Bandera, Texas

When John Crudder opened his eyes, light was pouring through the windows. He reached over to the other side of the bed but Charlotte was not there. John got up and slipped on his trousers and shirt and walked barefoot to the kitchen.

John called out, "Charlotte." But there was no reply. He looked through the house and realized he was the only one there. The twins' bedroom was empty and there was no one on the back porch. John took a seat on the porch, pulled on his socks and boots, and walked over to Slim's house.

He could hear the laughter of his daughters and smell biscuits cooking as he got closer. On the other side of Slim's house, John could see the dining hall. The last of the hands were walking out and saddling up for a day of work.

John's boots resounded on the porch. Charlotte met him as he was coming through the door. "Good morning, sleepy head." Charlotte kissed him on the lips and wrapped her arms around him.

"I can't believe I slept so long. Why didn't you wake me up?"

Charlotte kissed him again. "John, you needed the sleep. Your body knows what it needs. I'm glad we didn't disturb you."

Cora and Claire called out together, "Daddy!" They ran to him and hugged each of his legs. He bent down and scooped up a girl in each arm.

"We're cooking you breakfast," said Claire.

"I helped Grandpa make the biscuits," said Cora.

John walked into the kitchen and found his father-in-law, Slim and Richie, he had just discovered was the half-brother of Charlotte, busy but they didn't appear to be cooking breakfast. "Mornin', John," said Slim.

"Good mornin', Slim. Hello, Richie."

"Howdy," said Richie.

The kitchen was very large and had an island in the middle. There were pots and pans hanging overhead and cabinets and drawers under the work surface. There were piles of onions, bell peppers, and several heads of garlic. Slim and Richie were busy cutting up the vegetables.

John watched with curiosity as the two worked. "I know that's not for breakfast. What are you makin'?"

"We're gettin' ready for the fiesta," said Richie. "Today is Pa's birthday but it's also mine. We were both born on Independence Day. Charlotte had the idea that a good way to celebrate our birthday would be to have a fiesta and Pa and I would do all the cooking. After that, we'll all shoot off fireworks together."

"Happy Birthday, Richie." John put a hand on his shoulder and then put a hand on his father-in-law's shoulder. "Happy Birthday, Slim. From the looks of things, you must be planning on cookin' all day."

Slim wiped his arm across his forehead. "We've been at it since five o'clock and we'll need every minute between now and supper to get everything done."

"Breakfast is ready," said Charlotte. "You men wash up and come take a seat. John, you sit at one end of the table, and Daddy, you sit at the other end. Which of you girls wants to sit by Richie?"

"I do," said Cora.

"Then Claire, you come sit by me. Whose turn is it to say grace?"

"Daddy," said both girls as Richie and Slim pointed to John.

"You've missed your turn several times while you've been gone," said Slim. "John, it's good to have you back home."

"And it's good to be home, Slim. I've really missed all of you over the past several weeks. And I've missed our mealtimes. I guess I didn't realize how special this time has been to me until I was gone for the past two months."

"John," said Charlotte with a twinkle in her eye, "will you stop talking and start praying? We're all hungry."

The girls put out their hands and the whole family followed suit. John bowed his head. "Lord, it's good to be home. Thank you for my family and thank you for this food. Amen."

"And thank you for bringing my husband back safely,"

Charlotte added.

Bowls of food were passed around the table as Charlotte filled her daughters' plates. Slim got up, got the coffee pot and filled the cups. As John ate, he smiled at each member of his family and thought how fortunate he was.

When breakfast was over, Charlotte and the girls cleared the table while John washed the dishes. Richie and Slim went back to their fiesta preparations. "The girls and I are going to town to do some shopping," Charlotte said. "I'll get Owen to hitch up the buggy so you men don't have to stop what you're doing. Does anyone need anything from town?" The men shook their heads as Charlotte and the twins left the kitchen.

"I'm glad they left us alone for a while," said Slim. "I wanted to ask you about Granger and his gang, but I didn't want to do it in front of the twins."

"Slim, there are things he did that I can't even tell Charlotte. I didn't know people could be as evil as he is." Over the next several minutes, John went into detail about the grizzly crimes of Granger. Slim and Richie quit their cooking as they listened to John.

"I can't believe he would murder so many people," said Slim. "And it breaks my heart to hear what he did to that baby."

"Have you ever heard of anyone else using dynamite on people?" asked Richie.

"No, I haven't. And I have to say that there wasn't much left of the passengers on the stage. I'm just glad he's in prison. But it doesn't sound like it will be long before he stands trial for other murders. And one of the trials will be here in Bandera for murdering the Jacksons."

"Slim, how was Charlotte while I was gone?"

Slim thought for a moment. "Well, I know she missed you. But she didn't seem worried. You sending a telegram every few weeks helped her not to fret. She knows you won't take unnecessary risks."

"No, I won't. I have too much to live for—especially now. But I really hated to be gone so long."

"John," said Slim, "don't worry about Charlotte. She knew you were doin' what you had to do. And she also knows this won't be the last time you have to be gone."

"I guess you're right, Slim. Each time I've come back from a trip, I've thought it was my last one. I just appreciate you taking care of her and helping with the twins while I was away."

"I'm always glad to do that. And I think Cora and Claire enjoy their Grandpa time."

Roy Clinton

CHAPTER 2

Thursday, June 25th
New York City, New York

Bill Mosher had a gift. He was a boatbuilder from Long Island but found boatbuilding was a slow way to make a living. Mosher learned how to get money from others without having to work for it. Some would call him a criminal. His long police record attested to the fact that society at large didn't consider him a good man. But in Bill's humble opinion, he was a creative genius.

Mosher would use his boat in the waters around the city to prey on others. When he found a boat that was not occupied, he considered the owner had given him an engraved invitation to help himself to anything of value on board. He wasn't lazy. There were many days when he spent long hours scavenging—that's how he saw his larceny—and he never grew tired. He was intrigued by thoughts of possible treasure that awaited him as he boarded each vacant boat. And the potential of getting caught was his greatest thrill.

Mosher devised multiple con games designed to get people to part with their money. He may even have been the first one to try to sell the Brooklyn Bridge, which had been under construction for the previous four years. When he was not on his boat, he would spend his time looking for affluent homes he could burgle. He was equally as good at robbery on land as he was at sea.

For him to move up to bigger crimes, Mosher knew he needed an accomplice. That was especially the case now that the stranger had commissioned him to kidnap the child in Philadelphia.

Enter Joe Douglas. Douglas was a small-time thief. He didn't have much imagination. For that matter, he didn't have much intelligence. Joe was content to steal just enough to keep from having to get a job.

Bill spotted Joe picking pockets in New York City. He was amused at Douglas' clumsiness. What he learned from watching Joe was that he was fearless. He would get caught with his hand in someone's pocket one minute and then look for another victim the next. Mosher felt such a dimwitted person could be valuable to him. Douglas could be set up to take the fall if a crime went wrong.

Mosher approached Douglas in Central Park and confronted him. "I've been watching you pick pockets."

Douglas drew back. "What are you talking about? I ain't no thief."

"You're not a good one but you are a thief," said Mosher. "I've watched you for about an hour. You have gotten caught twice but you continue trying to pick pockets."

"I don't know what you're talking about," said Douglas.

"Don't get rattled on me. I'm not the law. What I am is someone who can make you a much better thief than you are now." Bill stuck out his hand. "My name is Bill."

Douglas looked at the other man skeptically and slowly extended his hand. "I'm Joe Douglas."

"Mr. Douglas, how would you like to have more money than you've ever made? I can show you how to make more money than you dreamed possible. All you have to do is work with me and do what I tell you to do."

Douglas hesitated, thinking somehow he was falling into a trap. Even if it was a trap, it was not one he could understand. Little did he know Mosher was planning on making him the patsy in his crime spree. If someone were caught, it would be Douglas.

"Well, what do you say? Do you want to join me or not?" asked Mosher.

"Yeah, I guess so. What have I got to do?"

"Well, the first thing I think we need to do is to find us a nice restaurant and have a good meal. And it's on me."

Douglas followed Mosher out of the park and across The Circle, down to Fifty-Sixth Street, and then across to Ninth Avenue. The sign on the front of the building said Tidewater Trading Post. "Don't let the sign fool you," said Mosher. "They have the best steak in town."

"I like steak," said Douglas. "I can eat a big one—that's if you're buying."

"I told you it was on me. Come on in. The sooner we eat, the sooner I can tell you my plan."

The pair took a table and ordered the largest steaks on the menu. When the meal was over, Mosher started telling his plan to Douglas. "There are some very wealthy people in Philadelphia who are going to be willing to give us some of their money."

"Why would they do that?" Douglas had a perplexed look on his face as he listened to Mosher.

"Because they're going to be grateful when we find their lost children."

Douglas listened but couldn't make sense out of what Mosher was saying. "How will we find their lost children?"

Mosher moved closer to Douglas and spoke in a whisper. "Because we're the ones who are going to take them."

Douglas' eyes grew large as he formed an 'O' with his mouth. Mosher continued to talk about the particulars of his plan as Douglas tried to take it all in.

"I guess there's lots of rich people here in New York. Why wouldn't they give us some money?" asked Douglas.

"Because we live here. We don't commit crimes like this where we live. We need to get away from here so no one will suspect we had anything to do with it. Let's get to Union Depot. There's a train leaving for Philadelphia later tonight. I want us to be on it. I'll fill you in on the rest of the details on the train."

They hired a buggy to take them to Grand Central Depot and by dusk, they were on their way to Philadelphia and would arrive by mid-morning the next day. Neither man had any luggage. Mosher said they would buy clothes when they arrived in Philadelphia.

Mosher eagerly shared his plans with the simple-minded Douglas. Douglas was fixated on only one thing: getting more money than he had ever seen in his life.

Roy Clinton

CHAPTER 3

Saturday, June 27th
Germantown, Pennsylvania

Christian Ross had all the trappings of wealth. He and his family lived in an affluent suburb of Philadelphia. His home was a mansion on a street filled with other mansions. From the outside, it appeared Christian was very wealthy. But the stock market crash the year before left him in dire economic straits. He had very little cash, all his investments had failed, and he was deeply in debt. Christian suspected many of his neighbors were also feeling the economic pinch. But appearances were important and he wasn't about to reveal his financial difficulties. Had he known what was going to happen, he would have gladly sold his house for a loss and moved to a modest part of town.

Mosher had a broad face with brown hair that had receded. His eyebrows were bushy. He had two very noticeable features. First, the cartilage in his nose was missing due to some past disease. Children said he had a monkey nose. Second, his mustache was snow white and connected with thick mutton-chop sideburns.

Douglas, on the other hand, was slim with a narrow face. His mustache was scraggly and black, matching his hair. His buckteeth made him an object of ridicule, not just when he was a child but throughout his life.

The men hired a buggy, and on their way to Germantown stopped at a clothing store to purchase several changes of clothes. Mosher didn't want anyone in New York to see them leaving town with suitcases. He gave attention to such details hoping no one would connect them to the crime he was planning.

Mosher drove up and down the streets of Germantown. It was completely within the corporate limits of Philadelphia. The whole neighborhood was filled with beautiful houses, but some streets had the largest ones. East Washington Lane had some of the nicer houses. All were set back fifty feet or so from the street and each had large yards of several acres. Each house had stables in the rear so most adults would enter and leave from the back of the house. But children loved playing in the front and side yards, where they could also see their friends.

Mosher handed the reins to Douglas so he could pay closer attention to the houses and select the right one. One house stood out. It was a two-story stone house with a cupola on top. Evergreen trees filled the yard. In front there was a stone wall and to the right of the house, there was an empty field of approximately three acres. Douglas stopped their buggy at the empty field and realized the trees completely blocked the view of the house.

Mosher smiled. "This is the house, Joe. Did you read the name on the wall out front?"

"I don't read so good," said Douglas.

"It says Mr. and Mrs. Christian Ross. Did you notice when we passed, there were toys on the front lawn?"

Douglas scratched his head. "No. But what does it matter?"

Mosher was beginning to get concerned that Douglas might be too simple-minded for the kidnapping. "Toys means kids. And we are looking for kids. Get it? We're going to kidnap a kid."

Douglas nodded his head in agreement. "How do we get the kids to come out to see us?"

"Right now," Mosher said, "we don't. Let's go back to town and get a room for the night. The next time we come back, we'll come back with lots of candy. When we see children playing, we'll offer them candy."

Douglas and Mosher continued down the street, and then turned and headed back to the center of the city, about seven miles away. They checked into a modest hotel and then walked to a store that was nearby and bought several bags of candy. The storekeeper was mildly amused at the sight of two grown men purchasing what was usually sold primarily to children.

That evening over supper, Mosher continued to talk of his plan to Douglas. "We're going to need some more men," said Mosher. "We need two more men to help us. I want to be able to watch the house and to follow Mr. Ross when he leaves the house."

"How are we going to find more men?" asked Douglas.

"The same way I found you." Mosher looked intently at Douglas. "If you wanted to find someone to help you with a crime, where would you go?"

Douglas thought for a moment. "To a park? Maybe find someone else picking pockets?"

Mosher smiled. "That's one place. Where else could we look?"

Douglas felt Mosher was giving him a test. And he knew from his failed attempts in school that he didn't do well with tests. "I guess we could look in saloons. Maybe we could spot someone who was cheating at cards."

Mosher nodded. "Very good. That is an excellent suggestion." Douglas smiled as he felt pride swelling within him. Mosher continued. "We could also go to the police station and watch for people being released from jail." Douglas nodded his agreement as Mosher pressed him further. "Of those choices, which do you suppose will give us the best results?"

Douglas thought again and tentatively responded, "Maybe the police station?"

Mosher nodded and smiled at Douglas. "I agree. Men just getting out of jail will be looking for a way to get back on their feet. Some of them will be looking for a way to make some easy money. After we eat, we'll go down to the police station and see if we can find some men to help us."

When their meal was finished, Mosher and Douglas took the buggy to the central police headquarters. The station was a large two-story building made of red brick. As was the case with many public buildings in Philadelphia, there was a cupola on top. They stopped their buggy, walked across and settled onto a park bench in front of the building. As the two men watched, they saw a parade of people entering and leaving the building. Some were policemen in uniform. Others were in handcuffs being accompanied by a police officer.

Several men were walking out of the station by themselves. Based on their appearance, Mosher judged some of them as just having been let out of jail. Mosher and Douglas carried on a running dialogue about the men. They took an informal vote between themselves as their potential coconspirators walked by. There were a significant number that both Mosher and Douglas rejected. Some were too old. Others seemed lazy and shiftless. And there were some who didn't appear to be intelligent enough to be much help. A few of the men looked good to Douglas but not to Mosher. One of the men appeared favorable to Mosher but Douglas didn't care for him.

After about an hour, a young man of about thirty years of age walked out of the station. He had sandy hair and was tall and slim. The young man paused on the steps of the police station as though he was wondering which way he was going to go. Mosher and Douglas looked at each other and nodded. This was their man.

As he walked away from the station, Mosher and Douglas fell in behind him. When they had walked about half of a block, Mosher called out to him. "We saw you coming out of the police station. Must have been rough in there."

The young man looked at Mosher and kept walking. Mosher called out to him again. This time he responded. "Yeah, it was rough. I've been in for six months."

"What'd you do to be locked up that long?" asked Douglas.

"I just robbed a couple of places. The bad thing is, I got caught."

"You looking for a job? Maybe we can help," offered Mosher.

"Is this some kind of a trap? Are you guys cops?"

Mosher and Douglas looked at each other and laughed. "No, we're not cops. We're needing some help on a job. We think you might be the guy we're looking for."

"What's in it for me?" asked the young man.

"One thousand dollars," responded Mosher. The three men walked quickly to the bench and sat down.

Douglas couldn't help but wonder what he was going to get. "Do I get a thousand dollars too?"

"Yes, you get a thousand dollars as well. But we need one more person to help."

"My partner gets out of jail tomorrow," said the young man. "He'll do a good job."

"What's your name?" asked Mosher, as he looked the young man over.

"I'm Harry. My friends call me Slick, 'cause I'm so good at taking things." Perhaps he wasn't so "slick" since he had been jailed for his past crimes.

"What's your last name?"

"Stegall. Harry Stegall."

Mosher shook his hand and then Douglas did the same as they

told Slick their names. Mosher pressed him about his partner. "Tell us about the man who gets out in the morning."

"His name's Rusty Rhodes. He's about my age. We knocked off a lot of houses before we got caught."

Mosher gathered his thoughts. "Do you think he'd be wanting a job when he gets out?"

"I know he would. Especially if it pays a thousand dollars."

"Where are you staying tonight?" asked Mosher.

"No place special. I was just planning on finding a bench in a park and staying there for the night."

"Let's go back to our buggy. We'll get you a room at our hotel. You can stay there," said Mosher. "Then you can go find Rusty in the morning and ask if he wants to join us."

"That sounds great," said Slick. "I've never stayed in a hotel before."

Roy Clinton

CHAPTER 4

Sunday, June 28ᵗʰ

Mosher and Douglas were eating breakfast in the hotel dining room when Slick walked in followed by another young man.

"This here's Rusty. He wants to join up with us." Rusty had bright red hair and a face full of freckles. He was as skinny as Slick and nearly as tall. His clothes were ragged and dirty.

Mosher and Douglas introduced themselves and shook Rusty's hand. "Slick, you and Rusty pull up a chair," said Mosher. "Your meals and rooms are on me."

Both young men took a seat as they were approached by a waitress. "May I get you gentlemen something to eat?"

Slick spoke up first. "I want scrambled eggs, bacon, sausage, pancakes, biscuits, and gravy."

"I'll have the same," said Rusty as both licked their lips.

"We didn't get much in the way of food in jail," offered Slick.

When the food was brought, both men devoured their food and ordered more. They didn't have any hesitation about eating so much since Mosher said he was paying. When they were finished, Mosher started giving them details on his plan. He told them about the kidnapping and the name of the child they were after. Mosher told them they would not get in a hurry and would be careful with every detail of the plan to ensure their success.

"Above all else, I don't want anyone to harm the boy in any way. He's no good to us if we hurt him. We need to be able to convince his father he is being well cared for and he will remain that way so long as he pays to get him back." The men listened attentively as Mosher talked. "I've got a telescope that we can use to find out more about the people who live in that house."

"You mean we're going to spy on them?" asked Douglas.

"Of course. How else are we going to find out when it's time to make our move? Douglas, the problem with you is that you've never planned out any of your crimes. When I was watching you in Central Park, you didn't even pay attention to who had money and who didn't. I watched you trying to pick the pockets of one man who was wearing a jacket that had holes in it. I'll bet he didn't have fifty cents to his name."

Douglas just nodded his head as Mosher continued. "I want to know everything we can about that family before we make our move. Tomorrow, I want us to be in the alley behind the house very early so we can find out more about the family." Mosher realized Douglas didn't appreciate the fine art of planning a crime.

"I've found out today that Christian Ross is supposed to send his wife and several of their children to Atlantic City. His wife has been ill and he thought it would be good for her to get away and a chance for the children to have a summer vacation. I want to make sure that happens. That'll only leave Mr. Ross and three of his children at home—and one of them is a baby."

Turning to address his newest recruits, Mosher continued, "Slick, I want you and Rusty to hire another buggy and keep watch on the house from the front. Don't get right in front. Stay off to the side, down the block and watch to see who comes and who goes. When Mr. Ross leaves with his family, Douglas and I will follow them to see where they go. Then, I want the two of you to move your buggy around to the alley and watch for Mr. Ross to return. This evening, we'll meet back here and tell what we've found out."

Slick and Rusty arranged for a buggy and went out to take up their position in the front of the house. Mosher and Douglas hitched up their buggy and went back out to Germantown. They found the alley behind East Washington Lane and stopped the buggy at the end, furthest from the Ross house and waited. Mosher used his telescope to get a closer view of the house but saw no activity. Meanwhile, they watched as stable hands at other homes hitched up buggies so their employers could go to work.

Although there was nothing nonchalant about the two men, they were out of place and more than one passing person regarded them with suspicion. Mosher grew impatient when there was still no movement at the Ross home by midmorning. They went out to the front of the house and saw Slick and Rusty parked down the street.

From what Mosher could tell, they looked like they were doing a good job of acting like they were not interested in the Ross house.

Mosher drove the buggy back down the alley and once again went to the far end and watched Ross's stable through the telescope. About noon, Mosher noticed movement. He could tell a very large buggy was being hitched. Soon, it was taken out into the alley and the family loaded up. To Mosher, it looked like a man and a woman and several children. From his distance, he couldn't tell what any of them looked like and he knew he was far enough from them they couldn't see him.

When the Ross buggy was a couple of blocks ahead, Mosher followed maintaining a discrete distance. The Ross buggy went to the train station with Mosher and Douglas trailing far behind. Mr. Ross had porters unload a large trunk and several pieces of luggage. Then Ross hugged his wife and the older children and watched them board the train.

Mosher knew the baby was back at the mansion with his nanny. He wished he was close enough to be able to clearly see Mr. Ross and the two younger children. But he wouldn't risk getting closer for fear of being discovered. He was content to know, just as the stranger in New York had told him, that later in the day, Christian Ross and the two younger children and a baby would be the only ones in the house. The fewer in the house, the safer he felt.

Ross and the two youngsters returned home followed at a distance by Mosher and Douglas. When the buggy turned into the alley, Mosher kept going and returned to the hotel. Soon, it would be time to meet up with Slick and Rusty. So far everything was falling into place.

Roy Clinton

CHAPTER 5

Monday, June 29th

Rusty and Slick were already in the dining room when Mosher and Douglas arrived. The two overgrown boys were busy stuffing their faces and hardly noticed when the two older men arrived. Mosher felt a bit like he was being taken advantage of but quickly put those feelings aside. He needed the two young men to successfully pull off the caper. Mosher and Douglas took their seats.

"I figured I'd find you two in the dining room," said Mosher. "Looks like you're enjoying the food."

Rusty swallowed and looked up at Mosher. "It's great. I love the food here."

"Me too," said Slick.

Mosher wasted no time in getting down to business. "What did you see while you were watching the house?"

Rusty was busy chewing so Slick answered. "We could see some people through the windows but we were far enough away that we couldn't tell anything except there were people in the house. When you left, we went around to the alley and parked at the far end. About an hour later, Ross came back and had two little boys with him. Once he went inside, we drove past the stable and saw a stable hand unhitching the buggy. We didn't see the little boys again. They must have gone inside. Then we just came back here."

"Did you see any other children on the street?" asked Mosher.

"There were a few," said Rusty. "But we didn't see any around the Ross house."

"Here's what we'll do." Mosher began laying out the plan for the morning. "Slick, I want you and Rusty to park your buggy down the street from the Ross house in the same place you were today. Douglas and I will park in front of the field next door. Your job is to keep a lookout for police or nosey neighbors. You'll not need to do anything except watch. If we need help, we'll signal you."

"What are we going to do?" asked Douglas.

"We're going to take the candy and hope the boys will want to play outside. I think they'll be curious enough about us they will come see what we are doing. I don't plan on taking them tomorrow. I want them to get comfortable with us so we can get them to leave with us in our buggy. It may take a few days to get them to that point."

The men nodded as Mosher talked about his plan. Then Slick

spoke up. "You said take them. I thought we were just going to snatch the youngest boy."

Mosher smiled. "I'm thinking we could get twice as much money if we take both boys. Besides, they'll probably be together. Charley is four years old. I'm not sure how old Walter is but he looked to be two or three years older."

"What if the boys don't want to come with you?" asked Slick.

"We'll worry about that when the time comes. If we play our cards right, they'll want to come with us. Boys like adventures. I'll just have to convince them we're going on an adventure and I think they'll come."

Roy Clinton

CHAPTER 6

Tuesday, June 30th

Early the next morning, Mosher and Douglas parked their buggy near the Ross house in front of the empty field. Slick and Rusty took up their place further down the block. The two teams were close enough they could see each other and signal if they needed help.

Around ten o'clock, Slick and Rusty raised their hands to get Mosher's attention. He didn't know what they were signaling about but he could tell they were excited about something they saw happening. Mosher couldn't see the house because of the thick trees. As he listened, Mosher could hear children playing. That must have been what Slick and Rusty were signaling about.

The boys burst through the trees. The little one was running from his older brother. The boys were laughing as they carried on their game of chase. "Hey Mister," said the older boy, "what are you doing?" Both boys were dressed in overalls and were barefoot.

The older one had short brown hair and was about six inches taller than his brother. Charley had blond hair that was long and curly. Mosher wondered if the boys would have been shoeless and in overalls had their mother been in town.

"Hello boys. My name is Bill," said Mosher. "And this is Joe. What are your names?"

"I'm Walter and I'm six." He turned to his little brother. "This is Charley. He's only four."

"Hello Walter. Hello Charley. Would you like some candy? We have a lot more than we can eat." Mosher stepped down from the buggy and held out the bag of candy.

"Sure, Mister," said Walter. "Can I have two pieces?"

"You certainly can. And Charley, you can have two pieces as well."

The boys happily helped themselves to the candy. "Bye, Mister," said Walter as they ran back to the house. The rest of the day, they didn't see the boys or any sign of Mr. Ross.

✳ ✳ ✳

For the next two days, both buggies were parked in the same place. The boys came out several times over those days and eagerly came to the buggy of Mosher and Douglas and happily accepted candy. They thought it was nice to have their new friends, Bill and Joe, give them candy. The boys got so comfortable they would climb up into the buggy to help themselves to the candy. They were especially excited to see Bill, and Joe had lots of different kinds of candy from which to choose.

Roy Clinton

CHAPTER 7

Saturday, July 4th
Bandera, Texas

Owen hitched the buggy for Charlotte and then lifted each girl onto the buggy bench. He took Charlotte's hand and steadied her as she got seated. "Thanks, Owen. Please tell Daddy that we'll not be gone long."

"You're welcome, Charlotte. And I'll pass along your message." Charlotte expertly maneuvered the buggy out of the barn and on to the road to town. Then she turned to her daughters. "You know what we're shopping for? We're going to get birthday presents for Grandpa and for Richie. What do you think they would like?"

Cora said, "A pony."

Claire agreed. "Yes, a pony."

Charlotte laughed. "I don't think either of them need a pony. Grandpa has a ranch that has lots of horses. He doesn't need a pony. Neither does Richie."

The twins looked at each other as they thought. "A buggy," said Claire.

"Yes, a buggy," said Cora.

"But we already have several buggies on the ranch. There's no need for another one. I was thinking maybe we could get them new hats. Do you think they would like that?"

"Yay! Hats," said Cora.

"We can pick them out," added Claire.

"We'll go to the store and pick out the perfect hats. Can you girls keep a secret? We want to surprise Grandpa and Richie during the fiesta."

"We won't tell," said Claire.

"It's our secret," said Cora.

Charlotte stopped the buggy at the general store. She helped the girls down and they immediately ran into the store and stopped at the display of candy jars.

"Good mornin' girls. Good mornin' Charlotte."

"Good morning, Mr. Anderson. I think every time we come in here, the girls head straight for your candy jars."

"Yes, they do, Charlotte. And they know I'll let them pick out one piece of candy each, so long as you approve."

"That's so sweet of you, Mr. Anderson. Yes, they can have one piece each, but no more."

Cora and Claire went from jar to jar trying to figure out which piece they wanted. They carefully compared their options and studied each jar carefully. Charlotte wanted to rush them but realized part of the fun was getting to decide which piece they got.

Her memory went back to her own childhood when she would come to the same store with her father and would pick out a piece of candy. Her father never hurried her. He allowed her to take all the time necessary to find just the right piece. Sometimes he would be through shopping and she still hadn't found the piece she wanted.

"Today is Richie and my father's birthday. I want to get them new hats. That is if you have any."

"I certainly do," said Mr. Anderson. "I have genuine Stetson hats made in Philadelphia by John B. Stetson."

"I don't know anything about hats. And Mr. Anderson, I just realized I don't even know what size hats they wear."

"That's all right, Charlotte. Stetson's have an adjustable hat band. They'll fit them perfectly. What color did you have in mind?"

"They both have straw hats that are pretty well worn. I was thinking they would both look nice in black hats."

Mr. Anderson smiled. "I think that's a good choice." He walked toward the back of the store. "Come this way, Charlotte."

She followed him and came to several shelves displaying hats. "On this row are all the Stetson hats. On this end are the least expensive ones. Down at the other end are the best."

Charlotte picked up a hat in the middle of the row and inspected it. "These don't look anything like the hats they wear now. Why are they so...flat? Don't you have anything that is more...stylish?"

Mr. Anderson chuckled. "These can all be customized to suit the owner. The brims are flat and the crown is straight with rounded corners. All they have to do is use a teakettle to steam the hat where they want to shape it. The steam softens the hat so they can bend it. Then when the hat cools off, it will retain its shape."

"That's amazing."

"And if they'd rather have me shape them, I'll be glad to. Just tell them to come by the store."

Charlotte put the hat down and moved to the end with the more modestly priced hats. She picked up the hat and inspected it. "This looks nice. In fact, I can't tell any difference in this one and the other one I was looking at."

"Actually, these are all fine hats. They're called the 'Boss of the Plains.'" He turned the hat over and showed her the sweatband. "Cowboys really like having a hat with Stetson written inside. These're known as the very best hats."

"How much is this hat?"

"It's five dollars."

"Five dollars!" exclaimed Charlotte. "I didn't know hats cost that much."

"I have other hats that are not as expensive but they are not Stetsons."

"No, I think you've sold me on getting them Stetsons." Charlotte moved back to the first hat she picked up. "How much is this one?"

"That one is fifteen dollars."

"My goodness. Why does it cost so much more?"

"If you'll look carefully, you'll see the material in this hat is much better quality felt than the other hat. Touch this hat and then touch the other one. You'll be able to tell the difference."

Charlotte carefully inspected the hat and then went to the hat on the end. "You're right, Mr. Anderson, I can tell the difference. I think I'd like to get this one for Richie. He's worth fifteen dollars." Charlotte giggled and added, "You know he is the only brother I have."

"Now I need to get Daddy's hat." She walked to the end of the shelf with the most expensive hat and picked it up. "Oh, my goodness. This hat feels wonderful. Is this fur?"

"Charlotte, you are very observant. That hat is made of pure beaver felt. It is the finest hat made. I've never sold one of these. I guess it is just too expensive for most people around here."

"I hate to even ask, but how expensive is it?"

"Prepare yourself, Charlotte. It is expensive but you need to keep in mind that it takes forty-two beaver pelts to make a hat like this." Mr. Anderson paused. "This hat is thirty dollars." Charlotte opened her mouth in shock and put a hand on her chest.

"I didn't know any hat cost that much." Charlotte carefully inspected the Stetson. She looked at the outside and then the inside. Then she started over again. Mr. Anderson wisely didn't talk while Charlotte continued to scrutinize every aspect of the hat. He knew he had made a sale. He just needed to let Charlotte come to that conclusion herself.

"Mr. Anderson, I'm going to take it. Daddy will be shocked if he finds out how much I paid for it. But he'll look so nice in it."

"I think you've made two good choices, Charlotte. And I also think it's an especially appropriate gift for Slim. After all, he is the mayor."

Charlotte laughed. "How right you are. Now we have to see if the girls know which candy they want," Charlotte said as she walked back to the front of the store. "Girls, it's time to decide which piece of candy you want. Have you decided?"

"Mommy," said Claire, "I want that one."

"And I want that one," said Cora. Mr. Anderson carefully fished the selected candy from the jars. The girls immediately put the candy in their mouths.

"Charlotte, I need to go to the storeroom and get boxes for the hats."

"That's fine Mr. Anderson. Do you mind if I leave the hats here for a few minutes? I wanted to go over and say hello to Clem."

"Certainly, Charlotte. I'll set them to the side. They'll be here when you're ready."

"Thank you." Charlotte left the store with a daughter on each side of her. "Stay right with me girls while we cross the street." When they got to the other side, the girls skipped down the boardwalk. They passed the livery stable and then went down to the marshal's office.

"Good morning, Marshal Williams." Clem looked up and smiled when he saw Charlotte.

He stood and took off his hat. "Hello, Mrs. Crudder. It's good to see you and the girls in town. What can I do for you lovely ladies?"

"Now what's with this Mrs. Crudder stuff. You know I've always just been Charlotte."

"I know, Charlotte. And I've always just been Clem."

"Yes, I like that better. Clem, we just stopped by to invite you to supper tonight. It's Richie and Daddy's birthday. They're home cooking right now and will probably be cooking all day."

"I'll be glad to come. I didn't have any other plans."

"I'm glad. We're having a fiesta. And you better come hungry. With those two cooking, there's sure to be lots of food."

"That sounds like my kind of party. I'll be there just as soon as I close the office."

"Bye, Clem. See you tonight. Come on, girls."

Charlotte retraced her steps back toward the general store. As they passed the livery stable, the owner tipped his hat to Charlotte and continued nailing a sign to the front wall of the stable. "Hello, Mr. Harris. What are you doing?"

"Hello, Charlotte. Girls." He stepped out of the way so Charlotte could read it. It said Free Puppies. "That old dog of mine just had a litter of puppies. You don't know of anyone who needs a dog, do you?"

"We do," said Cora.

"Yes, we want a puppy," said Claire. Charlotte giggled for she could have predicted her daughters' response.

"No, girls, we don't need another dog around the ranch. But we can go pet them if you want to."

The girls squealed with excitement and followed Mr. Harris back deep into the stable. "They're so cute," said Charlotte. "What breed are they?"

"Well, the mother is a Golden Retriever. It's anybody's guess what else the pups have in 'em. But they look much like their mother did when she was a puppy."

Charlotte picked up one puppy and petted it. "How old are they?"

"They're about a month old. I wanted to keep them with their mother for a month. But now it's time to find home for all six of the little guys."

Claire and Cora knelt, gently petting each of the puppies. "Mommy, you should get one for Richie," said Cora.

Charlotte pursed her lips as she considered what Cora said. "Mommy," said Claire, "Richie would really like a puppy."

"Girls, I think you're right. That would be a great present for him. Let's get a little boy puppy for him."

"I'm certainly glad to part with one," said Mr. Harris. "But I'd like it even better to be parting with two of them.

Cora stood up and tugged at her mother's dress. "Mommy, if we're real good, can we get a puppy, too?"

"Yes, Mommy," said Claire. "We'll be real good. Can we have one, please?"

Charlotte resigned herself to being outvoted. "I guess so. What do you want; a boy or a girl?"

"A girl!" said both girls at the same time.

"Mr. Harris, one more puppy if you please. And make this one a girl."

Mr. Harris laughed. "I'm sure glad you ladies came by this morning."

"I am too," said Charlotte. "Can you girls carry the puppies? Be very careful. We have to go get our packages from Mr. Anderson. Thank you, Mr. Harris."

Charlotte helped the girls into the buggy and then picked up her purchases from the general store. All the way back to the ranch, Charlotte smiled as she watched her daughters playing with the puppies. "What are you going to name your puppy?"

Cora and Claire looked at each other and shrugged their shoulders. "I don't know. What are good doggie names?" asked Cora.

"I know," said Claire. "She looks like an angel. Let's call her Angel."

"Yay," said Cora. "Angel is a pretty name."

"I think that's a fine name," said Charlotte.

"What are we going to name Richie's puppy?" asked Cora.

"Don't you think we should let Richie name his own puppy?"

The girls nodded and kept petting the pups. When they arrived at the H&F Ranch, Charlotte left her packages in the buggy. The girls climbed down and carefully carried the little fur balls into the house. "Grandpa, we got a puppy," said Cora.

"Richie, you got a puppy, too," said Claire.

Richie and Slim came out of the kitchen to see what the twins were so excited about. They smiled as they saw the puppies and joined the girls in petting them.

"This is Angel," said Cora. "She's a girl."

"And Richie, you get to name your own puppy. And he's a boy," Claire added.

Richie laughed. "Well thank you. I've never had a puppy

before. I'll have to come up with a good name for him."

"Well, Richie, if we're gonna get the food ready in time, we need to get back to the kitchen."

"We got you another present," said Cora.

"But we can't let you see it. It's a secret," said Claire.

CHAPTER 8

Wednesday, July 1st
Philadelphia, Pennsylvania

T he four kidnappers gathered in the dining room for breakfast. There was an air of excitement for they all knew the time for the kidnapping was growing closer. Mosher assumed his place at the end of the table. Their food was served and no other guests were nearby.

"All right, men. Today's the day." The other three men stopped eating and stared at Mosher. "There has not been any change in routine over the last few days. Mr. Ross has not left the house and the boys are spending a lot of time playing outside. What I'm confident of is that we will not have to enter the home to take Charley. He will willingly come with us."

Slick and Rusty resumed eating after a few seconds. Douglas seemed to be carefully weighing Mosher's words. But Mosher knew it was not deep thoughts Douglas was having. He was more than likely contemplating what he was going to do with his share of the money.

"As I said earlier, I think it will be easier to take both boys. Charley will be more likely to go with us if Walter is already in the buggy. Besides, with two boys, we may come out of this richer than we've expected."

Slick put down his fork, swallowed the food he had just stuffed in his mouth, and weighed in. "How do we know Mr. Ross is even going to be there today? I mean, he could get up this morning and go to work and take the boys to a relative's house."

Mosher smiled. "I think he's taking off the entire week. If he didn't go into the office Monday or Tuesday, I don't think he will go for just one or two days. I wouldn't be surprised if his office is closed on Friday."

"How would you know that?" asked Slick.

"I don't know it but I think there is a good possibility that may be the case. Saturday is a national holiday and I think many businesses will give their employees Friday off."

"I didn't know Saturday was a holiday," said Douglas.

Mosher enjoyed showing the other men how much more knowledge he had than they did. "If you men would read the newspaper, you would have known that four years ago, Congress declared the Fourth of July a national holiday. The same bill declared Christmas as a national holiday."

"But Christmas has been around all my life," said Rusty. "I remember getting Christmas presents when I was a little boy."

"I didn't say Christmas started four years ago, but that it was made a national holiday then. That means most businesses and schools are closed." Mosher looked down at the table and collected his thoughts. "So, back to Ross. I think he's going to be home all week which means the boys will be there as well."

"What are we going to do after we take them?" asked Slick. "We can't bring them back here."

"I've got that all worked out." Mosher pulled a map from his pocket and laid it out on the table. "After we snatch the boys, we have to get them away from this area. Slick, you and Rusty will take the boys to a cave I've found. I've already got it stocked with food, and the other supplies you'll need. All you have to do is take them there and then you get to relax. You just have to babysit until their father pays to get them back. It will take you less than two days to get there."

Slick and Rusty exchanged a look. Slick spoke up. "Are you crazy? How will we ever keep the kids quiet that long?"

Mosher smiled and pulled a brown bottle from his pocket. "This is chloroform. Just a few drops on a cloth and get the boys to breathe it and they will go to sleep. Only use it when you absolutely need to."

The other men smiled as they thought how easy the crime was going to be and how much money they would get for a few days of work. They continued eating their breakfast in silence. When they were through, they went outside and hitched their buggies.

"One more thing," Mosher said to Slick. "You'll need some expense money for your trip and while you are taking care of the boys. Here's one hundred dollars. That should be enough for anything you need over the next few days. Before you leave, buy some extra food from the kitchen and you can take a bag or two of candy with you."

Slick had a wide smile when he took the money. "Thanks, Bill. You've thought of everything. I like working with someone who is such a good planner."

Mosher smiled to himself as he turned to go back to his buggy. Little did the others know he hadn't done much planning at all. The plan was laid out for him and the expense money had been provided by the stranger. The cave stocked with supplies, the chloroform, even the selection of the Ross home, had all been the plan of someone else. Mosher didn't mind taking credit for it. He believed he deserved the credit since he was the one taking all the risks.

The buggies pulled out one after the other. After a couple of blocks, Slick and Rusty turned onto a side street to allow Mosher and Douglas to get farther ahead. Both buggies continued to Germantown and down East Washington Lane. Mosher's buggy was already in place in front of the empty field when Slick and Rusty arrived. They parked down the block as they had for the past several days. Once in position, Slick gave a little wave to Mosher.

In the middle of the morning, Mosher heard children playing. This time, the boys wasted no time in their own yard but made a direct path toward what they had come to think of as the candy wagon. Walter came running through the trees as he shouted back at Charley. "You better hurry, Charley. The Indians are gonna catch us. We have to get away in our wagon."

Walter didn't even wait for an invitation but climbed up into the buggy and hid under a blanket he found on the floor behind the seat. "Come and find me, Charley. I'll bet you don't know where I am."

Little Charley came running after his brother but not soon enough to see where Walter disappeared. "Walter, you better come out. Hey Mr. Bill, did you see where my brother went?"

Mosher smiled and pointed to the blanket in the buggy. "No, Charley, I don't know where he went. But you better get up here before the Indians catch you." Charley smiled and accepted help from Mosher to get into the buggy. "Why don't you hide under the blanket so the Indians can't find you."

Charley did as was suggested and laughed with glee as he discovered his brother. Mosher gave the reins a pop and the buggy started down the road. Slick and Rusty immediately moved in directly behind Mosher's buggy.

"Hey, Mister Bill," said Walter. "Where are we going?"

"Have you gotten any fireworks yet? You know the Fourth of July is coming and you need to have some firecrackers and some of those sparkler sticks. Would you like to go get some?"

"Yeah, that would be fun. Hey, Charley. Let's go get some fireworks. We can really play cowboys and Indians if we have some firecrackers." Walter climbed up on the buggy seat between Mosher and Douglas. Charley soon followed and both boys laughed and talked about how much fun it was going to be to have their own firecrackers.

What Mosher had not counted on was how crowded the buggy seat was with both little boys joining them on what was meant for only two adults. He was also not prepared for how rambunctious Walter could be. No sooner had Walter gotten on the buggy seat than he jumped up, went under the seat to the back of the buggy, and was making pretend gunshot sounds. "Hey, look," yelled Walter. "There are Indians behind us. I'm going to shoot them. Pow. Pow. Pow, pow, pow. Come help me Charley. We've got to kill the wild Indians."

"Hey boys," said Mosher, "don't do that. Quiet down and come back up here." Mosher's plea went unheeded. Both boys continued their attack on the trailing buggy. The buggies continued out of the Germantown neighborhood. Fortunately, Mosher didn't see anyone taking special interest of them.

"Listen to me boys!" Mosher's voice became noticeably louder and much more gruff. "If you want to get some fireworks you have to settle down."

"I want to go home," cried Charley. "I want to see my daddy."

"Now, son." Mosher put on his most soothing voice. "You'll get to see him in just a few minutes. We will get the fireworks and then you will be able to go home. Look! That store has a sign that says they sell fireworks. Walter, would you like to go in and pick out what you want?"

"Yay! Will you give me some money?"

"I sure will." Mosher plunged his hand into his pocket and came out with a quarter. "This will buy you and your brother a lot of firecrackers. We'll wait here while you pick them out."

Mosher watched as Walter climbed down and went into the store. Once they could no longer see him, Mosher popped the reins several times and moved the horse into a trot. Slick and Rusty stayed right with them. He admonished himself for thinking they could ever pull off a kidnapping with two boys. He was not only doubling their risks but the presence of a second boy all but assured their crime would not be successful.

As the buggies moved away, Mosher congratulated himself on changing his plan on the fly. Walter would find his way home while the four men concentrated on Charley. That was turning out to be a greater challenge than he had anticipated.

Charley, who was still whimpering, began to cry in earnest. Mosher said, "Get that baby on the seat between us and keep him quiet."

Douglas slid around on the buggy bench and grabbed Charley and pulled the screaming boy to the front of the buggy. He roughly put him down on the seat beside him and yelled, "Shut up!"

Mosher whipped the horse into a gallop and soon they were clear of the houses of Germantown. Slick and Rusty were trailing close behind. Soon, they were clear of any buildings and out in the countryside with no signs of other people. Mosher pulled his buggy well off the road into a grove of trees and stopped. Slick followed suit, climbed down, and ran up to Mosher's buggy, followed by Rusty. Slick handed over a rag on which he had poured chloroform. "Here use this."

Mosher put the rag to the boy's lips and Charley immediately quit crying. The men looked at each other and smiled. "That was quick thinking, Slick. Let's get him back into your buggy. But keep the chloroform close so you can use it if he starts throwing another fit."

Douglas carried the boy back to the other buggy. They laid him on the floor in front of the buggy seat and covered him with a blanket. Mosher looked at Slick. "You've got the map, don't you?"

"Yes, sir. I've got it."

"Then get going. If you make good time today, you should easily make it there by evening. Don't waste any time. And don't stop around other people. We don't want that brat calling any attention to what you're doing."

Slick and Rusty climbed into their buggy and continued down the same road. Rusty took the reins and Slick consulted the map. It looked like they would continue down the same road to the northwest. The map showed several roads that appeared to be nothing more than horse trails. Hopefully, they would find the cave before nightfall.

Mosher turned their buggy around and trotted the horse back to their hotel. All the way, Mosher smiled as he congratulated himself on a well-executed plan. Douglas nervously kept looking back, wondering if they were going to get caught.

CHAPTER 9

Saturday, July 4th
Bandera, Texas

I f I could have everyone's attention." John raised his voice above the lively conversation in Slim's living room. "Hello! Hello!" Finally, the crowd of friends stopped talking.

"I wanted to say something on behalf of Slim and Richie. We're glad you've come to join us for this Independence Day celebration. But this is also the birthday of Slim and Richie, and this is a different kind of birthday. We asked each of you to come with empty hands and a good appetite.

"This is not a day for presents for the birthday boys. Instead, they have a present for us. They've been cooking all day, preparing a fiesta for us. I'm gonna ask Slim and Richie to tell us what they've prepared."

Slim stood, smiled, and cleared his throat. "This has been an interesting day. I've done a bit of cookin' through the years. But to be honest, no one has accused me of being a good cook." The room erupted in laughter. "And as much as I love Mexican food, I've never cooked much of it. Fortunately, Richie is not only an excellent cook but his best dishes are Mexican. About all I can tell you is we are havin' beans, rice, and enchiladas. I did make the beans, mashed 'em up, and then fried 'em. Richie said they're called refried beans—but I only fried 'em once. I've told you all I know. Richie, stand up and tell us what else we're havin'."

"Pa's bein' modest. He's a great cook. In fact, he's almost as good as my Ma was." Richie choked up a bit as he thought about his late mother. "I was in the kitchen cookin' with her ever since I can remember. In fact, we cooked supper together every night."

Richie saw Slim wipe tears from his eyes as he thought about his love for Marie and the life they could have had together if he had only known where to find her. Marie broke off her relationship with Slim before he knew she was expecting because she knew her very proper Castilian parents would never accept her marrying a gringo.

"What Pa said is true. We're havin' refried beans, Mexican rice, cheese enchiladas, beef enchiladas, beef tacos, tostadas, and salsa picante. I think that's about it."

The group applauded and remarked at how they looked forward to the meal. Charlotte stood and took command of the room. "Before we eat, the girls and I have a couple of presents to give the birthday boys." On cue, Claire and Cora came in holding the puppies. "This morning, the girls picked out a new puppy for themselves and brought Richie one as well. They named their puppy Angel. They were going to name Richie's as well but they decided to let Richie do that. Richie, have you come up with a name?"

"I think I'll call him Buster."

"That's a great name, Richie. And there's one more gift for two of my favorite men." Charlotte slipped over to the storage area beneath the stairs. "Daddy, Richie, I know you both have hats. In fact, you both have several. But you don't have a real Stetson." She presented each with his new hat to the "ooh's" and "ah's" of the guests.

"For you ladies, these are just regular hats. But what the men know is that Stetsons are the finest hats made, I wanted the special men in my life to each own one." She caught herself and looked at John. "And not forgetting one more special man in my life. John, I guess I sort of obligated myself to make sure you get one as well."

Everyone laughed at Charlotte's faux pas. "All right folks, I guess it's time to eat."

"Before we eat," Slim said, "I would like to say a blessing. If you would please stand." Everyone stood and held hands with the people beside them.

"Dear Lord, we're grateful for the way you've blessed us. As I look around this room, I see friends I've known all my life, and others I have known only a short while. I'm grateful for my family. I've been so richly blessed. Thank you for the food you've given us. I hope nobody gets sick from my cookin'. A-men." Several people chuckled.

Charlotte stepped forward and gave directions. "Go into the kitchen and grab a plate. All the food is set up on the counters. After you fill your plate, you can eat at any of the tables set up in here or the kitchen. And when you eat all that's on your plate, go back and get a refill. There's plenty."

After a few minutes, plates were filled and the assembled crowd was well into their first rounds of food. Charlotte heard someone riding up so she went to greet the new guest. Marshal Williams trotted his horse to the hitching rail, swung down, and walked up to the porch. "Evenin', Charlotte. Is there any food left?"

"Of course, there is, Marshal. Come on in. We've just started."

He walked into the living room. "Howdy, everybody. I shor hope there's some food left 'cause I'm powerful hungry."

"Howdy, Marshal," said Slim. "Fill your plate and then come join us at our table." Clem wasted no time filling his plate and taking the empty seat. After several bites, he spoke up.

"I almost forgot. I've got two telegrams for John. Let me find 'em. Here they are." Instead of handing the telegrams to Crudder, he cleared his voice and read the first one out loud.

John Crudder
Bandera, Texas

Fredericksburg courthouse money to be delivered by stage. Alvelda is healing nicely. Sends her love.

Howard Hastings

Fifth Avenue, New York City

John smiled as he thought about the surprise that would soon arrive for his friend in Fredericksburg. When he heard of Alvelda's continued recovery, he let out a sigh of relief. Then Williams read the second telegram.

John Crudder
Bandera, Texas

Come immediately. Bring MM.

Jeffrey Jameson
Washington, D.C.

Clem continued eating as he finished reading the second telegram. In between mouthfuls, the marshal looked over at Crudder. "John, who do you know in Washington, D.C.? And who's MM?"

Charlotte and John exchanged a look as Slim tried to change the subject. "Charlotte, why don't you refill the Marshal's plate? Do you think you have room for seconds, Clem?"

Roy Clinton

CHAPTER 10

Wednesday, July 1st
En Route to the Cave

During the first hour of their trip north, Slick and Rusty settled into a routine they would follow for the rest of their journey—actually for the rest of their time with Charley. Rusty proved to be the better one relating to the young boy. When just a boy himself, he had been tasked with taking care of three younger brothers by his single mother. It wasn't a matter of wanting to help his mother or of being the "man of the house," it was simple necessity since the only job his mother could get was serving drinks in a saloon.

Rusty's mother would get them up in the morning, fix them breakfast, and assure her four sons that she loved them. But for all practical purposes, Rusty raised his siblings. He collected his brothers after school, made sure they did their homework, fixed them supper, and got them to bed on time. He demanded they obey him. There were even times when he would spank them. He didn't resent his role in the family. He was just doing what needed to be done. In the process, he found he had a knack for both keeping his brothers entertained but also of relating to them when they were sad, lonely, mad, or rebellious. His good humor ended many a fight. His even-temper helped him win arguments. And his sense of propriety prevailed when there was any defiance. But there were still times when he would lose his temper with them and spank them so hard he left marks on their backs and bottoms.

When Charley began to regain consciousness, he was confused by his surroundings and the lack of familiar faces. Rusty picked him up and held him in his lap while Slick drove the wagon. This suited Slick fine. He didn't mind doing all the driving so long as he didn't have to deal with "the Brat." Rusty admonished him for his name calling.

"So long as you call him names or treat him gruffly, he'll be scared and will probably cry," said Rusty. "You don't have to like him. Just don't treat him like he is your enemy."

"I'm not treating him like that." Slick took offense to Rusty telling him how to do his job. "I'm just not good at taking care of little kids."

"You do the driving and I'll tend to Charley. Remember, he's worth a whole lot of money to us, so we've got to take good care of him."

"I want to go home." Charley's voice was weak as he came out of the fog caused by the chloroform. Rusty instinctively rocked him back and forth.

"You're going to have a great adventure," Rusty said. "Slick and I will take good care of you until your parents get here. Then we will all have a great adventure together. My name's Rusty and I know your name is Charley. What's your full name?"

"I'm Charles Brewster Ross. Mom says when I grow up, everybody will know my name."

"Why is that?" asked Slick.

"'Cause I'm gonna be famous." Charley rubbed his eyes and remained lethargic. "She said I'm gonna be a banker or a lawyer."

Slick laughed but he sounded more derisive than amused. Rusty bounced Charley on his knee trying to get him to fight off the effects of the sedative. "I'll bet you'll be a good banker," Rusty said. "And you can be a lawyer, too."

"I want my mommy. I want to go home." Charley started crying. Soon his cries were loud and unrelenting.

"Keep that brat quiet," said Slick.

"Don't call him that." Rusty hugged Charley tightly and rocked him but his crying continued unabated. Slick gritted his teeth in an effort to remain silent and not further upset the boy.

"When are we goin' home? I want my mommy."

"We're gonna have a great adventure," said Rusty. "You just wait and see." Rusty's voice remained calm as he tried to talk to Charley between his screams.

"It's a good thing no one else is around," said Slick. "We'd have to make other arrangements if there was anyone else on the road." Rusty wasn't sure what he meant by "other arrangements" but he shuddered at the thought. He made a mental note that he would take care of everything concerning Charley so Slick wouldn't lose his temper.

After what seemed like an hour but was in reality only about ten minutes, Charley's cries became little more than a whimper. "What kind of adventure?"

Rusty said, "We're gonna get to go camping and explore a real cave. Tonight, we could even sleep out under the stars if you wanted to. And tomorrow, we get to go fishing. Have you ever been fishing?"

Charley sniffled. "No. I don't want to go camping. I want to go home."

"It'll be fun," said Rusty. "And your mommy and daddy will even get to come and visit you and go fishing. Would you like that?" Rusty did all he could to find something that would appease their young prisoner. He would promise him anything to just get him to remain quiet.

"I want to go home." Charley's voice wasn't nearly as strong as it had been earlier. His crying had left him tired. For that, Slick was grateful. The miles dragged by as Charley continued asking questions and Rusty tried to placate him. Slick just drove the buggy and wondered if snatching the boy was really such a good idea.

At midday, Slick pulled the buggy off the road near a stream and rested the horse. Charley had finally fallen asleep on the floor of the buggy, exhausted from his crying. Rusty let him sleep and climbed down, first going to the back of the buggy and collecting the food he had bought that morning. After eating, both Slick and Rusty lay in the shade of the buggy and fell asleep.

Slick awakened suddenly and realized Charley was not in the buggy. "Get up, Rusty. The brat is gone."

"What do you mean, gone?" Rusty rubbed the sleepiness from his eyes. "I left him sleepin' in the buggy."

"Well, you may have left him there, but he's not there now. Get up and help me look for him. If he's gotten away, Mosher is going to be angry at both of us. It was your job to keep watch on him. My job was driving. All you had to do was watch out after the brat."

"Quit calling him that. Call him Charley." Rusty jumped on his feet and brushed the dirt off his trousers. "He can't have gotten far. You go that way. I'll look over here."

The men spread out and searched through the weeds calling out Charley's name over and over. Slick picked up a stick he used to thrash the weeds to see if they could be covering where Charley might be hiding. "Come on out, you little brat," said Slick. "You can't hide from us. I'm gonna find you and you'll be sorry."

"Charley, please come out," said Rusty. "I've got some biscuits and ham for you. You haven't eaten so I know you're hungry."

How could a four-year-old boy have just disappeared? He couldn't have gotten that far but the two men searched diligently and couldn't find any trace of Charley. They searched for half an hour, looking in all directions and still they couldn't find him.

"Let's follow the stream," said Rusty. "Maybe Charley walked along the water's edge. You go north. I'll go south." Rusty and Slick took off walking as fast as they could along the stream. The weeds were not thick right up next to the bank. They hoped

Charley had simply followed the stream and was still walking.

Nearly a half mile from the buggy, Slick spotted Charley walking along the stream. When Charley saw him, he started running and crying as he ran. "Come here, you little brat. I'm gonna teach you not to run away." When Slick caught up with Charley, he tore a switch from the branch he was using to move weeds in his search. "Come here and get what you deserve."

Slick caught up with Charley and grabbed him by the hair and started whipping him with the switch as hard as he could. Charley started screaming and Slick continued hitting him. With each lash, Charley screamed louder. Slick's switch connected with Charley's back and legs. Several lashes were on his arms and at least one left an angry welt on Charley's face.

Rusty heard Charley screaming and ran as fast as he could in the direction of the sound. When he arrived, he saw Slick repeatedly hitting Charley with the switch. He ran to Slick and took the switch from his hand and then hit him as hard as he could in the mouth. Slick let go of Charley's hair and turned toward Rusty in a rage. He pulled back his fists to fight but Rusty stepped to the side and hit Slick hard in the stomach. Slick doubled over and Rusty brought his fist up and into Slick's nose. Immediately, blood began to gush from the broken nose as Slick fell backwards.

Slick gathered himself and as he was standing, he kicked Rusty and landed a foot into his ribs. The blow was so powerful that Rusty went down. While he was down, Slick stood over him and kicked him repeatedly. Rusty rolled to get away from Slick, got to his feet, and landed blow after blow with his fists into Slick's face and gut. Finally, Slick sank to the ground and held his arms out to ward off any further attack. "No more. I can't take no more."

Rusty stood over his partner in crime with his fists doubled up. He looked down at Slick as he paused to catch his breath. "What were you thinking, Slick? You can't beat the boy like that. Mosher told us he was not to be harmed in any way. Mosher might kill us for disobeyin' orders."

"I didn't hurt him. I just gave him a good lickin'. Every boy gets a lickin' when he's bad. And Charley shouldn't have run off. He deserved it. And he ain't hurt none."

"Just look at him," shouted Rusty. "He's got welts on his arms and legs. And his face is bleeding where you switched him."

"Like I said, he ain't hurt none. A lickin' does a boy good every once in a while."

"Slick, you better hear me on this. If you hit that boy again—if you hurt him in any way, I'm gonna kill you."

Slick dropped his eyes so he was no longer looking into the face of the man who had soundly defeated him. "I won't hurt him. But remember, he's your responsibility. You take care of him so I won't have to."

"I will, Slick. If you want to receive your part of the ransom, you have to do your part of the work. But if you harm him…." Rusty's word trailed off as he glared at the man he had once trusted.

Charley's cries had become whimpers. Rusty walked over to the boy and picked him up and started walking him back to the buggy. He hugged the boy and carried him all the way back. At the buggy, Rusty pulled down Charley's overalls and lifted his shirt. He couldn't believe how many welts the boy had on his back and legs. Silently, Rusty made a vow that once they had delivered Charley back to his home, he was going to kill Slick.

Rusty got Charley some ham and biscuits. The little boy ate hungrily. Slick climbed up in the buggy and guided it back onto the road. Charley no longer sat between the two men. Rusty had moved over next to Slick and put Charley on his right side. He was determined not to let Slick hurt him again. Slick didn't say anything for several hours. Charley spoke only to Rusty and did so in a whisper. Occasionally he would cry but for the most part, Charley didn't utter a sound.

Charley's running off put them behind schedule. They had to accept the fact they would not make it to the cave by the end of the day. That was just as well for they didn't want to try to find the cave in the dark.

When evening came, Slick guided the buggy off the road. He didn't stop until he was several hundred yards away from any potential traffic. He built a fire while Rusty engaged Charley in gathering more firewood. Rusty made it a game to see who could gather the most. Charley got fully engaged in the game oblivious to the fact that he had been savagely beaten just a few hours earlier.

Slick put a pot of coffee on and got out the remaining ham and biscuits. They ate in silence and before long Charley was nodding off. "Come on with me, Charley," said Rusty. "I'm gonna make you a bed in the buggy. You'll be safe up here. And if you need anything during the night, you just wake me up. I'll be sleeping right out here beside the fire."

Charley seemed comforted by Rusty's promise. "Rusty," said Charley, "would you tell me a story? My mommy always tells me a story when I go to bed. And my daddy tells me a story when my mommy is gone."

"Sure, I'll tell you a story. What kind of story would you like?"

"I want a story about me."

Rusty chuckled. "All right. One story about Charley coming up." Rusty thought for a moment and then began his tale. "There was once a little boy named Charley. He lived with his mother and daddy and his sister and brothers in a big house in Germantown, Pennsylvania. His father was very rich and well-liked by everyone in the town. Charley's mother was very pretty and a very good cook. She made all of the things that her husband and children liked to eat. She made fried chicken, and pot roast."

"And corn on the cob," said Charley.

Rusty laughed and continued. "And corn on the cob, and cornbread, and biscuits, and ice cream."

"Yes, ice cream. Charley loves ice cream."

"One day, Charley met a new friend named Rusty and he took him on an adventure. He took him on a long buggy ride and they camped beside a stream. Then he took him to a secret cave in the woods and taught Charley how to fish and Charley caught the biggest fish anyone had ever seen. And then Charley went home and told his mother and daddy and sister and brothers about his adventure and how he had become a great fisherman."

"Rusty, is it fun to fish?"

"It sure is, Charley. You'll find out. So, he told his family what a great fisherman he had become. And then Charley grew up and became a very famous banker. Everyone knew his name. In fact, the whole bank was named for him. Anytime someone came into the bank, they would see the sign above the door, 'Charles Brewster Ross Bank.' And everyone who came in the bank would want to meet Mr. Charles Brewster Ross because he was such a great man. And that's the end of the story."

"You forgot to say 'and they lived happily ever after.'"

Rusty smiled, "And Charley and his family all lived happily ever after. The end."

Charley clapped. "I liked that story. Tell me another one."

"Not tonight, Charley. I'll tell you one tomorrow night. Right now, you need to get to sleep." Rusty picked the boy up and placed him on the floor of the buggy. He was asleep shortly after Rusty covered him with the blanket.

"Why are you coddlin' the boy like that?" asked Slick.

"I'm not coddlin' him. What I'm doing is makin' our job easier. If he's mad at us or scared of us, we are going to have a harder time. The best thing we can do is to make him feel like he's on vacation. I'll do whatever I need to in order to keep him happy. Besides, it'll make the time pass much faster." Rusty poured himself another cup of coffee. "How much longer do you think it will be before we get to the cave?"

"As best as I can tell, we have five or six hours more in the buggy. We can't go as fast as I would like with just a single buggy horse. Tomorrow, we need to find some place to buy some more food. All we have left is some bacon. That'll do for in the morning but we will need something to eat later in the day."

"Slick, I'm sorry I beat you up. But I just can't take it when I see a child being hurt."

"I didn't hurt him, Rusty. He just got a good whippin'. Didn't you ever get a whippin' when you was a kid?"

"I did some. But I didn't like watching you whip him."

"Well, I still don't think I hurt Charley."

Rusty turned so he could face Slick. "You can go on believin' what you want to believe. But I'll say this. You better not raise a hand to him again or I guarantee you'll regret it."

Roy Clinton

CHAPTER 11

Wednesday, July 24th
Washington, D.C.

C rudder headed to Washington D.C. the morning after the fiesta. There was no question in Charlotte's mind that he had to go. She knew the telegram from Jeffrey Jameson was actually from President Ulysses S. Grant. She assumed John would once again be pressed into service as a special emissary of the President.

John made it to San Antonio in time to catch the afternoon stage to Kansas City. He stabled Midnight at the livery in San Antonio and paid extra to make sure that his special horse was groomed every day, exercised some, and got plenty of oats. The stableman recognized John from previous trips and readily agreed to give Midnight the extra attention.

The stagecoach made it to Kansas City in two weeks. John thought how much warmer it was than when he had taken this trip the year before in the late Fall. In Kansas City, Crudder boarded the train for New York City and then took another train to Washington D.C.

When he arrived in the nation's capital, John went immediately to the Executive Mansion and presented himself to the doorman. He was ushered into the massive lobby to wait for the President. John didn't have to wait long for the President to greet him.

"Mr. Crudder." The President coughed as he puffed his ever-present cigar. "So good of you to visit me."

John thought that was an odd response. The President acted as though John had a choice in the matter. But Crudder was very clear he had been ordered to appear before the President.

"It's good to see you again, Mr. President. And please just call me John. Thank you for seeing me."

"It's my pleasure, John. Come on back to my office." John followed the President into the President's office. President Grant motioned to one of the upholstered chairs arranged in front of his desk. John recalled, when he was there previously, the only furniture in the room was the President's desk and two couches that had been pushed against the walls. Even with the addition of the chairs, the office was a great expanse of unfilled space.

The President took a seat behind his desk and continued puffing his cigar. He looked across at John as though he was gathering his thoughts. After several seconds of silence, he finally spoke.

"John, I have to congratulate you on the work you did with Carmichael and Summerall. You took care of the problem and made sure they could not continue taking the country into financial ruin. Unfortunately, they'd already badly damaged the economy not only of our nation but of the world. What we don't know is how much worse it could have been without your help."

"Thank you, Mr. President. I appreciate the confidence you placed in me and I'm glad you were pleased with my work."

"You're welcome, John. What I realized during that time you were acting as my Special Agent is that I needed someone like you that I could call on from time to time. I always knew there would be a day when I needed to call on you again. Well, that day is now."

"I'm at your disposal, Mr. President. How may I be of service to you?"

"I'll get to that in a bit. What I want to know is if you would like to enter into a more formal relationship with me?"

"I'm not sure what you mean, Mr. President."

"What I mean is, how would you like to continue being Special Agent of the President of the United States?"

"Well, Mr. President, while I am flattered by your confidence in me, I'm not sure I'm the right person for the job."

"Nonsense."

Crudder wasn't sure how he was to respond. He opened his mouth to speak but couldn't find words that seemed appropriate. Trying again, John said, "Mr. President, I can't see how a rancher can be of much service to you."

"John, you have all of the qualities that make you ideal for this job. And bear in mind, we're not talking about a full-time job or you relocating to the District. You'll still be able to live on your ranch and enjoy family life. And for the most part, I'll try not to ask you to travel too far from your home. The current case is an exception. I needed you here but that will not always be the case."

John opened his mouth to speak but the President waved his hand indicating he was not through talking.

"As I was saying, you have the qualities that make you ideal for my purposes. You know the law. Your Harvard Law School education is, in my opinion, the finest education available. And I like the fact that you have served as a marshal. That gives you a unique perspective and I know you approach things from the standpoint of how justice can best be served."

"Thank you, Mr. President, but…"

"John, just rest easy. I'll let you know when I'm through and I want a response. Now let's talk about the Midnight Marauder. Your experience in this area gives you the incomparable credentials for the job. But it is more than being able to bring a swift end to those who are beyond the law. Your sense of justice and of right and wrong help you hold in check your prodigious ability with your fists, your knives, and guns."

John opened his mouth to speak when, once again, the President held up his hand to silence him.

"And, John, I know you are also a man of restraint. When you dealt with Roger Quarles Mills, you showed control a lesser man would not have shown. I wouldn't have faulted you if you had ended the life of that pompous blowhard. But instead, you gave him a chance to change. And, from what I have been able to learn, he's changed significantly."

This time, John was too stunned to respond. He was sure his

face showed a mixture of fear and concern. What did the President know and how had he gained that information?

"John, I didn't summon you here to cause you any trouble. I know you are wondering how I know you're the Midnight Marauder. But I wouldn't be much of a Commander in Chief if I didn't know about the capabilities of my troops. I've spent years as a soldier and a leader of men. You have abilities that are unmatched. And your small stature causes people to underestimate you—and that's also an asset.

"Now I don't want you to think you don't have a choice. I'm quite serious when I say if you want to decline my offer to help your President and be of service to your country from time to time, you can walk out of this office and never hear from me again. And I'll do everything in my power to protect your secret."

Crudder looked at the rug beneath his feet and tried to make sense of his thoughts and feelings. He raised his head to speak but then closed his mouth and let his eyes go back to the floor.

"Mr. President, everything inside me tells me to decline your offer as graciously as possible. But I also know you would not call on me if you didn't believe I could be of help to our country. When you called on me last year, I was at a loss to know how I could help but then found I could make a difference.

"Ever since I was a boy, I've had a deep desire to right the wrongs I've seen. Then in law school when I first got acquainted with the statue of Lady Justice, it was clear to me that I want to see the Scales of Justice balance. And, in all candor, when I first came to grips with the fact that sometimes I'd need to step beyond the bounds of the law to make that happen, I was at peace. At the same time, I have a deep belief that so long as I can work within the law, that's what I must do."

The President nodded his head. "I have already heard about the man you brought in to stand trial in San Antonio. With all the people he's killed, you would've been fully justified in ending his life. That's just one more example of why I think you're the right man for this job."

"Mr. President, I'm pleased to accept your offer to help you when you call on me. And I appreciate you saying it wouldn't be often and that you would try to assign me to cases that are closer to my home."

"I'm glad to hear that. I knew I made a good decision asking for your help. Raise your hand and repeat after me:

"I, John Crudder, solemnly swear I will support the Constitution of the United States and faithfully execute the orders of the President of the United States."

John repeated the oath as directed. President Grant then picked up a piece of paper lying on his desk and handed it to John. "Read this. If you agree with what I have written, I'll sign it. And I have already prepared a copy for you that I'll also sign."

To Whom It May Concern:

John Crudder of Bandera, Texas, also known as the Midnight

Marauder, is hereby appointed as Special Agent of the President of the United States of America. Furthermore, he is directed to use any measures he deems necessary, up to and including lethal force, to accomplish his mission for the President of the United States. Additionally, he is pardoned for any and all past crimes he has committed or may have committed.

Ulysses S. Grant
President of the United States
of America

John couldn't believe what he was reading. He never dreamed he would receive a pardon for things he had done as Midnight Marauder. Not only that but the President had basically given him a license and directive to kill if it was called for. As he thought about that, rather than feeling relief that he could operate with impunity as the Midnight Marauder, he felt a greater burden and new resolve to only use deadly force if he believed a criminal was beyond the reach of the law.

"I've been meaning to ask, how are Charlotte and the twins doing?"

Once again surprise registered on John's face. He was amazed at how much the President knew about his personal life. "They are doing just fine, Mr. President. Thanks for asking."

Grant let out a great cloud of smoke from his cigar and began a deep, hacking cough. "Now let's get down to business. I didn't get you here just to make you my Special Agent. And by the way, from now on, when I need you and you make your reports, I want to do it by letter. That will save you traveling back here."

"I appreciate that, sir."

"The reason I called you here is because an unprecedented crime has just been committed. On July 1st, a four-year-old boy was kidnapped from his home in Philadelphia. A few days later, the father received a letter demanding he pay twenty thousand dollars for the boy's return. Never before has there been a kidnapping for ransom in our country. I want you on the case. Find the kidnappers and bring that boy home. It is crucial that we end this quickly before other criminals decide this is a good way to make money."

Over the next few minutes the President laid out the facts of the case. John listened intently. At times he paused and took notes so he would have addresses as well as the names he needed. He asked several questions to make sure he had all the information necessary. Toward the end of the conversation, John got the President to reiterate his mandate.

"That's right, John. You have my permission and direction to use deadly force as needed. You decide when that time is. Basically, I want you to continue to be the Midnight Marauder but do it for your President. One important consideration is the impact a prolonged criminal trial would have on the country. I'm not sure that would be good for our country."

John thought for a moment. "I can certainly see your perspective, Mr. President. I'll not forget that when the time comes."

The President handed Crudder a second letter he could present to any authorities on this or other cases that said he was the Special Agent of the President. He also gave him a wallet that contained a badge and an identification card that was signed by the President. John thought about how many times he had declined to carry a badge for fear it would restrict him from the work he needed to do. He stared at the badge that was made especially for him. A large gold star was surrounded by a circle of writing: *Special Agent to the President: John Crudder*. He realized this badge didn't limit him but rather empowered him like no other badge could.

Grant abruptly stood and extended his hand. John then realized the meeting was over, just as suddenly as his first visit was several months earlier. John followed the President out to the lobby where the doorman opened the door and quickly closed it as John walked out onto the colonnade. John put his hat on and stood in stunned silence as he replayed the remarkable meeting that had just ended. He looked at the copy of his pardon and directive to use deadly force if necessary. Crudder realized he was likely the only person to possess such a document.

Roy Clinton

CHAPTER 12

Wednesday, July 1st
Germantown, Pennsylvania

Christian Ross' concern over finances caused him to make even deeper cuts in the household staff. That morning, he released one of the nannies, the cook, and the gardener. He reasoned he could rehire them at the end of summer or whenever his financial circumstances changed.

"Walter! Charley!" Christian walked all around the house looking for his boys. Where could they have gone? He knew they liked playing in the field next to their house but they were forbidden from going anywhere else. He went out the front door to look for them.

"Walter! Charley!" Christian shouted. "You come home this instant. You don't want to make me come after you."

Christian walked out to the street and looked back at his house. He was sure the boys were hiding somewhere nearby. As he looked at the house, he recalled Walter had once crawled under the house so he went back and found the place where he had caught Walter. Getting down on his knees, Christian looked under the house. It was sitting on blocks so he could see all through to the other side.

"Walter! Charley! Are you under here?" Christian moved down the side of the house, looked under again and called for his sons. He repeated this until he had gone completely around the house.

He went back to the street and walked down several blocks, paying careful attention to the yards. Christian looked up each tree thinking it would be just like the boys to have chosen one to climb. He went up one side of the street and then down the other. There were no signs of his sons.

Christian knocked on the doors of his neighbors asking if they had seen his sons. He was sure someone had seen something. He reminded himself he needed to be persistent. Christian continued going from neighbor to neighbor. Finally, he knocked on the door of Mary Kidder.

"Miss Kidder, I'm sorry to bother you. But have you seen my sons? Charley and Walter are missing. I know they play in your yard some."

"Hello, Mr. Ross. Yes, I've seen them. They rode off with some men about two hours ago. I thought they were relatives because the boys climbed up into their buggy like they knew them."

Christian Ross grew excited. "What did the men look like?"

"Well, one of them had long bushy sideburns and a funny-looking nose." She looked from side to side as though she didn't want to be overheard. "I think he must have had a disease. His nose just didn't look natural."

"What about the other man?"

"He looked tall and slender. Now mind you, he was sitting down so I couldn't tell how tall he really was. But he did look like he was a tall man. His face was narrow and his teeth stuck out and he had a big gap between his two front teeth."

Christian turned and ran down the steps. Then he turned back. "Thank you, Miss Kidder. I don't mean to be forward. You have been very helpful. When you see the boys again, please tell them to get home immediately."

Christian ran back to his house and out to his stable and quickly hitched his horse to his buggy. He slapped the reins on the horse's rump and set out down the street.

"Charley! Walter!" Christian shouted at the top of his lungs again for his sons. He went down his street for a mile or more, whipping his horse the whole way. Every few seconds he shouted his son's names. He turned the corner, went over a block, and then headed down that street to the end. Then he went over another block and followed it to the end.

As the hours passed, Christian's voice grew hoarse from shouting. He kept watch for his sons and especially noticed the occupants of every buggy he passed. When he would pass someone walking on the street, he would question them about a buggy containing two men and two boys.

Desperation grew as the hours passed. Mr. Ross felt helpless as he continued his search. He didn't feel any closer to finding the boys but knew he couldn't stop. What was he to do? How was he ever going to find them?

Not knowing anything else to do, Ross turned his buggy toward downtown Philadelphia. He had passed the central police station several times through the years but had never had need to go there. He searched his memory trying to recall the address of the station but to no avail. Up one street and then down another, Ross methodically searched central Philadelphia until he found the imposing brick structure.

He pulled his buggy to a stop in front of the station and jumped out without even tying his horse. Running inside, he shouted as loudly as he could, which was nothing more than a gravelly whisper.

"Help me! Somebody help me! My boys are missing!"

A uniformed policeman approached him. "Hey, mister. What's all the commotion about? Why are you so excited?"

"You've got to help me. My sons are missing. You've got to find them."

"Settle down, mister. Come with me. We'll go to the back of the station and you can tell me what's going on."

Christian did his best to be patient but he couldn't understand why the policeman didn't seem to have any sense of urgency. The policeman led Christian to an office at the far end of the station. "Sir, you can come in here and take a seat. I've got to get some paper so I can take your report."

"Report? I don't want to give a report. I want you to find my sons."

"Now settle down, sir. We're going to find your sons but you must settle down. The first thing we need to do is to get a report of all the pertinent details. Take a seat. I'll be right back."

The policeman walked out as Mr. Ross did his best not to be anxious. Rather than sitting down, he walked back and forth through the office, pacing from one side to the other. After what seemed like an eternity but was in reality not much more than ten minutes, the policeman returned followed by two more policemen.

"Now, Mister—Mister—I never did find out your name, sir?"

"My name is Christian Ross."

"Pleased to meet you, Mr. Ross. I'm Sergeant Dixon. This is Corporal Rubins." Then, indicating the third policemen who was dressed in street clothes, "And this is Detective Ramsey."

Ross nodded at the three men and shook the hands that were offered. "Mr. Ross, you said you needed help finding your sons. Please tell us what happened."

"I was working at home this morning and Walter and Charley—that's my boys—were playing outside like they always do. I started to miss them when I realized I hadn't heard either of them for maybe an hour or more."

"Is that uncommon?" asked Sergeant Dixon.

"Not really," responded Mr. Ross. "They play outside like lots of boys. I don't usually worry about them because they stay nearby. But then I remembered my wife was out-of-town. She usually keeps track of them when they're playing."

"And where is your wife, Mr. Ross?"

"What does it matter? I want you to find my sons. Why aren't you more concerned about them?"

"I understand your concern, Mr. Ross. Please believe me when I tell you we are concerned and want to find your sons. But panicking is not going to help. Please try to calm down and just tell us what happened."

"Panicking? Yes, I'm panicking. My sons are missing. How do I get through to you men?"

"Just try to remain calm, Mr. Ross, and tell us what happened next. When did you realize your sons were missing?"

Christian took several deep breaths and tried to contain his anger. "I'm sorry. I know I seem unreasonable. I'm just so worried about my sons."

"That's all right, Mr. Ross. Now you said your wife was out of town. Where is she?"

"She's taken most of the children to Atlantic City for summer vacation. She's just been gone a few days. Walter and Charley are scheduled to join her there in a couple of weeks. Anyway, when I remembered she was not at home to look after the boys, I went outside and called them. They usually come immediately. Where could they have gone?"

"Take it easy, Mr. Ross. I know this is a trying time for you. So, you said you called them. What did you do then?"

"I kept calling them. They always play in our yard or in the empty lot next to our house. But they always come when I call them."

"What did you do when they didn't come?"

"I went out into the yard and called them even more loudly. I cupped my hands to my face and called."

"I'm sure you called them many times. After you called them, what did you do?"

"I went up and down the street knocking on neighbors' doors— asking if anyone had seen my boys. That's when I got to Miss Kidder's house. She said she had seen them get into a buggy with two men."

"When did that happen?"

"She said it was a couple of hours prior—no, maybe she said it was one hour—I don't know what she said except she saw the boys get into the buggy like they knew the men."

The policeman used his most solicitous tone trying to get Ross calm enough to recall the details. "Mr. Ross, is it possible they went for a ride with a neighbor, especially since Miss Kidder said she thought the boys knew the men?"

"I don't know. How am I supposed to know? They've never done anything like that before. Where did they go? It's been at least five hours, maybe longer. Where could they be?"

"We're going to find them, Mr. Ross. We've never had a case where missing children didn't show up after a little while. Now, what neighbors were your sons close to?"

Ross looked off into the distance as he thought. "I guess they knew most of our neighbors. We've had most of them to the house at different times—some for dinner—others for parties. The boys always liked the attention they got from adults. Sergeant, do you think one of the neighbors has taken them?"

"Well, I don't think anyone has taken them. But I do think it is most likely your sons are at a neighbor's house having tea and cookies."

"That's just absurd," shouted Ross. "They've been gone all afternoon and it's almost dusk. They're not having tea and cookies and they're not at any neighbor's house. I've checked with all of them."

"Now, now, Mr. Ross. I didn't mean to upset you. It's just that in cases like this, we find missing children are with neighbors or have gone to a relative's house. Do you have any relatives in the area?"

Ross leaned forward and put his head in his hands. "Sergeant, aren't you going to go out and find my sons?"

"Mr. Ross, what we are doing right now is for the purpose of finding your sons. You yourself have already experienced the futility of aimlessly knocking on doors and asking if anyone has seen your sons. We must conduct a proper investigation. While answering my questions may not seem like it's helpful, it'll ultimately assist us in determining our next steps."

"I'm sorry, Sergeant. I'm just so worried about them. They've never done anything like this before." He paused, bowed his head, and began to cry. "Please, Sergeant Dixon. Tell me what I'm supposed to do."

"You're doing just fine, Mr. Ross. Just keep answering my questions. You are really helping me get the proper focus for the rest of our investigation. I just have a few more questions. Then I think it's best for you to go home before it gets dark. Your sons are probably waiting there for you now."

Ross wiped his eyes. "Do you really think so?"

"I certainly think it's possible. Anyway, I think what looks like a mystery will be solved and we'll find out it was no mystery at all."

"I hope you're right."

"I know I am. Just a few more questions, Mr. Ross. Have there been any strangers in your neighborhood recently?"

"Strangers? You mean maybe a stranger took my sons?"

"That's just it. We don't know. We must check on every possibility. Have you noticed any strangers around your house or in your neighborhood?"

"No. I haven't seen any strangers. I mean, occasionally there will be a drummer or peddler come by but we shoo them away."

"What about your servants? Have any of your household staff seen strangers around your house? Have you questioned your gardener and stableman?"

"Sergeant, I've not seen anyone around our house or neighborhood who didn't belong."

Roy Clinton

CHAPTER 13

As he sat in the police station, Christian thought how incongruous it was for him to have a mansion and not have a houseful of servants. He recalled how only a year and a half before, his household staff had numbered ten, counting the upstairs maid, the downstairs maid, the cook, two nannies, his wife's dresser, the butler, who also doubled as his gentleman's gentleman, two gardeners, and the stableman.

But he remembered so very well how quickly life had changed for him on the day the stock market crashed on September 18, 1873. Prior to that, Christian felt he was set for life. He had more money than he could spend in several lifetimes. He had enough resources to set up each of his children in business and leave them an inheritance that would see them through to old age.

Only his wife knew of what he liked to call his "financial problem." In reality, it was not a problem but a full-scale disaster. His associates still saw him around the office, dressed in his dapper best. The neighbors noticed he drove himself to work instead of being chauffeured by his stableman. Only one person had even commented on that and Christian told him that he missed caring for his own horse and buggy. He waxed eloquently about how it took him back to fond childhood memories.

He had not told anyone—no one at his office, no neighbors, and certainly no relative—that he had let the staff go, one by one, because he simply didn't have money to pay them. Christian Ross felt like a failure. While he didn't cause the stock market crash, he should have been wise enough not to have placed all his resources in it. The day after the crash, he realized he had less than one thousand dollars to his name. For someone of more modest means, a thousand dollars was a handsome amount of money. But for a man with such a large estate and such significant living expenses, a thousand dollars was a paltry sum.

While the financial world went into a panic, Christian Ross had his own private terror. With the loss of all his investments and no way to replace them, he was faced with some very tough decisions. Actually, his decisions were not so tough at all. One if his largest expenses was his household staff. He let the maids and the stableman go on the day after the crash. Within a couple of days, he terminated one of the landscapers and the cook. The next day, his wife's dresser was relieved. The following day, he released his butler. He still employed one nanny and a gardener. He felt he had to keep the yard well-manicured as long as possible to keep up appearances.

Over the past several months, he pressed his older children into yard service to help the single gardener. One neighbor had noticed and he quickly extolled him with the importance of instilling a work ethic into each of his children. He would join them in the yard and act as though he was excited about working alongside them and showing them not only the value of work but the joy in it. Christian smiled to himself at the memory.

✳ ✳ ✳

Sergeant Dixon called Ross's name twice before he was able to rouse him from his thoughts. "Mr. Ross, what's wrong? I have been talking to you but you don't seem to be hearing me."

"I'm sorry, Sergeant. I guess I was just thinking about my children. I'm so worried about them."

"I understand, Mr. Ross. Now I was asking about strangers. Have you noticed any strangers around your house?"

"Like I said, there have been a few but they don't stay around...." Ross stopped midsentence and lifted his head. "But there was the Candy Man."

"The Candy Man?"

"I don't know why I didn't think of that before. Walter—he's the older of the missing boys—had some hard candy a few days ago. I asked him where he got it and he said the Candy Man gave it to him."

"Who's the Candy Man?"

"Sergeant, that's just it. I don't know. In fact, at the time, I didn't think any more about it. I just thought one of the neighbors gave Walter some candy." He paused again, deep in thought. "We have such a nice neighborhood. Everyone is so friendly and helpful. I didn't give it another thought. This may sound bad but I was thinking more about business and not paying close attention to the boys. I was glad someone was nice to them. And Walter seemed happy to have the candy."

"What day was that?"

Christian Ross paused and thought. "I guess the first time was three—no four days ago. That's right. The first time I saw him with candy was on Saturday."

"The first time? Mr. Ross, why didn't you tell me about that earlier? This is important. How many times did you see your son with candy?"

"I don't know, Sergeant. I guess it was every day since Saturday. Do you think the Candy Man took my sons?"

"Don't get excited, Mr. Ross. We're going to find out. I just wish we had this information an hour ago. Did you ever see the Candy Man?"

"No. Like I said, I thought a neighbor had given the boys candy."

"Now think, Mr. Ross. When Walter told you about the Candy Man, where did he say he saw him?"

Ross looked from side to side and got very excited. "He said he was in a buggy in front of our house."

"Did you see a buggy in front of your house?"

"No, I didn't. But you don't understand. I have a large yard and there is a wall in the front. And our yard is filled with trees. From the street, it is difficult to even see the house. That's one of the things we love most about it. We're nestled in behind our wall and trees and are pretty much cut off from the surrounding houses. Everything is so quiet in our neighborhood."

"So, you didn't see the buggy Walter told you about? And you didn't see the Candy Man?"

"No, Sergeant, I didn't. I know that makes me seem like a bad father. But I'm really a good father. I am always there for my children. In fact, I have been working from home for the past week since my wife has been out of town. I wanted to be near my boys. I could have gotten a sitter for them, but I wanted to be there for them."

As Ross spoke those words, he got lost in his own thoughts again. Was that really why he was working from home and had not hired a sitter? He knew it was not true that he just wanted to stay home with the boys, but it was part of the fiction he told everyone. He wouldn't admit to anyone his financial circumstances had changed so drastically. And he was so wedded to the idea that things had not changed financially, some of the time, he found he forgot about the dire financial straits he was in.

"What else can you tell me about the Candy Man?"

"I don't know anything more. I just know Walter said the Candy Man gave him candy. I didn't even think anything about it. What kind of a terrible father am I that I didn't see the danger of that man? I didn't give him another thought."

"Take it easy on yourself, Mr. Ross. I don't fault you in the slightest. In fact, I don't think I would have responded any differently if my own son had told me he got candy from someone. Did Walter give you any additional information about the Candy Man?"

"I'm sorry, Sergeant. I don't remember him saying anything else. I asked him where he got the candy and he just said, 'The Candy Man gave it to me.'"

"Did he say anything about the buggy? Did he say he got into the buggy?"

"Sergeant, he didn't say *anything* else. I've told you everything he said."

"I know you're growing impatient with my questions, but it is crucial we gather all the information we can."

"I know that, Sergeant. I just want my boys back. If I knew anything else, I would tell you."

"Very well, Mr. Ross. I think we can call it a day. We have all the information we need to get started bright and early in the morning."

"In the morning? Are you crazy? My boys are little. They've never been alone at night. Either my wife or I are with them every night. We have to go look for them now!"

"Mr. Ross, you are not being helpful right now. We are doing everything we can to find your sons. In the morning, we will organize a search and muster all our forces. At this time of day, we are not going to have the resources to begin a full-scale search. I will be sending out several officers to search through your neighborhood and question your neighbors. And when the late shift reports to work, I will personally give them the information we have now. I don't mean to imply that we're not going to do anything tonight. In fact, I plan on working throughout the night to get things organized so a search can begin in earnest in the morning."

Ross hung his head. "Thank you, Sergeant. I didn't mean to suggest you weren't doing your job. I realize you're doing all you can. What am I to do? I don't want to go home. There's no way I can sleep tonight. I just don't know of anything else to do."

"The best thing you can do is to go home and try to remember anything else that might help us find your sons. Write down your thoughts and your memories. Something may come to you. And do your best to get some sleep. I want you to be rested tomorrow as we get the rest of the search in progress. Meanwhile, I'll get all of the available manpower out searching now."

"Thank you, Sergeant."

"Now, go home, Mr. Ross. Get some rest. Have a meal. And be sure to leave your doors unlocked. Your sons will likely come home this evening and you want them to be able to get into your house."

"You're right. I'll bet they'll come home tonight. In fact, they may have already come home and are looking for me."

"That's the spirit. Go home and wait for your boys to get there and tell you of their great escapade."

Roy Clinton

CHAPTER 14

Wednesday, July 1st

C hristian Ross walked out of the police station feeling lost. For a moment, his hopes were buoyed as he imagined his sons waiting for him at home. But as he got into his buggy, he felt utterly helpless and lost. Where could his sons be? Why would they have gotten into the buggy with anyone? And even if they took a ride, why have they been gone so long?

These and dozens of other questions went through his mind as he considered the void in his life. At least if his wife was home, he would be able to talk with her and they would be able to comfort one another. But with her recent illness he didn't believe he even wanted to bother her with the boys' disappearance. There was certainly nothing she could do and he didn't want to make her health worse by having her worry about something beyond her control.

Christian turned the buggy toward home and got his horse into a trot. He thought he needed to get there soon in case the boys were home. Within a few minutes, Ross left downtown Philadelphia and was on the way to Germantown.

He was lost in thought and not paying much attention when he heard a familiar voice.

"Daddy! Daddy! That's my daddy." Ross looked around trying to locate the source of the voice. Across the street, he saw a man holding Walter by the arm while Walter was crying and struggling with all his strength to get away.

Christian stopped his buggy in the street and ran across to his son. As he got close Walter broke free and ran to his father. "Daddy! I'm scared. Daddy!" Walter's face was stained with dirt that had been interrupted by trails of tears.

Ross gathered his son into his arms and hugged him tightly. "Walter, where have you boys been?" Then he turned his attention to the man and responded with an outburst of anger. "What have you been doing with my son?"

"Hold on there, mister. I haven't done anything to your son. I found him crying and saying he was lost. All I did was try to keep him out of the street so he wouldn't be run over. I asked him where he lived and he said, 'at home with Mommy and Daddy.' If my son was wandering along a busy street, I'd want someone to help him."

"I'm sorry, sir. I had no right to get angry with you. I'm indebted to you for what you've done for him."

"I'm glad I could help. My name is Peacock. Henry Peacock."

"Glad to meet you, Mr. Peacock. My name is Christian Ross. This is my son, Walter. Where is Charley?"

"Who?"

"My other son, Charley Ross. Where is he?"

"I'm sorry, Mr. Ross, but I don't know."

"Walter, where is Charley?"

"I don't know, Daddy. I guess he is with the Candy Man."

"What do you mean he is with the Candy Man?"

"Well, we were going to the store to get some firecrackers."

"Firecrackers?"

"The Candy Man said he would take us to get firecrackers and some other stuff."

"Have you been with the Candy Man all day?"

"No sir. We went to the store a long time ago. Charley was crying saying he wanted to go back home but the Candy Man and the other man said we were going to get firecrackers first."

"So, what happened? Why isn't Charley with you?"

"I went into the store to get the firecrackers. The Candy Man gave me a quarter and told me to pick out what I wanted. I got a lot of firecrackers and had four cents left over. When I came back outside, they were gone."

"What do you mean they were gone?"

"The buggy was gone and so was Charley and the Candy Man."

Ross grabbed Walter by each of his arms and raised his voice. "Where did they go?"

Walter started crying again. "I don't know, Daddy. They were just gone. I don't know where they went."

"Walter, it was your job to watch your brother. You're the big brother. Why didn't you watch him closer?"

Walter cried in earnest. "I did, Daddy. I watched him all the time. He was fine when I went into the store." Walter rubbed his eyes as he cried. Mr. Peacock stood by awkwardly and watched the exchange between the distraught father and his son.

"Walter, if you had been watching him like you were supposed to, Charley would still be here."

"Now, listen here, Mr. Ross. I don't think it is fair for you to take it out on Walter. Look at him. He is terrified. He's been lost and through an awful ordeal and now you are blaming him for losing his brother. What kind of father are you?"

"I'll thank you to mind your own business, Mr. Peacock. I'm sure I know what's best for my son. Please butt out. You're not welcome in this conversation."

"You are some miserable excuse of a human being. That's the thanks I get for trying to help Walter find his home."

Ross relaxed the hold on Walter's arms and stood up. "I'm sorry, Mr. Peacock. I appreciate you helping Walter. I'm so glad he is safe. I'm just worried about little Charley. He is only four years old. I don't know what to do."

"I realize you're distraught, Mr. Ross. At the risk of being told once again to mind my own business I am going to say one more thing before I go. Walter is not at fault for Charley being missing. If there is anyone who's at fault, I would suggest you look a little closer and see if you can't find a more obvious choice."

"You're right, Mr. Peacock." Turning to Walter and stooping

down to his level, Christian said, "I'm sorry, Walter. It is not your fault Charley is lost. It's my fault. I should have been watching the two of you closer. If I had, you never would've left with the Candy Man. Please forgive me." He pulled Walter in close and hugged him and joined the little boy in crying. After a full minute, Christian stood and extended his hand to the stranger who had gone out of his way for a lost little boy.

"Thank you, Mr. Peacock. I owe you a great debt of gratitude. I have no excuse for my behavior. I hope you'll forgive me for being short with you. If not for you, I would not have Walter back with me."

Henry Peacock took Ross's hand. "You're welcome, Mr. Ross. As a father, I can only imagine how you must be hurting right now. I have no hard feelings. And I hope you find your son very soon. Please give me your address. I'll check in with you in the morning. If Charley is not at home, you can count on me to help you find him."

Ross took a business card from his suit coat and wrote his home address on the back. "Thank you, Mr. Peacock. I would certainly appreciate your help. I don't know the first place to look for Charley. I've just come from the police station. They assured me they've already begun searching and will mount a full-scale effort tomorrow."

"I'll see you in the morning, Mr. Ross. We're going to find your son. I just know we will."

"Thanks again, Mr. Peacock."

Christian picked up Walter and carried him to the buggy. As he sat his son on the buggy seat, little Walter rubbed his eyes. Christian took his place beside him and put a comforting arm around his son. "Let's go home, Walter. We need to get there so we can let your brother inside when he gets there." He popped the reins on the rump of his horse and urged him home.

"I'm hungry."

Ross turned to his son. "That's right, you haven't had your supper."

"I haven't eaten anything since last night."

"Didn't you eat breakfast?"

"No. Me and Charley ran outside to play as soon as we got home."

"Why didn't you eat breakfast?"

"You never make breakfast. Mommy makes us breakfast. But she's not here."

"Walter, I'm so sorry. You're right. I haven't made you breakfast all week. It didn't even occur to me. Please forgive me. I'll get you home and make you something just as soon as we get there."

CHAPTER 15

Thirty minutes later, Christian turned into the alley behind his house and pulled the buggy up to the stable. He climbed down and then lifted Walter out of the buggy. Ross left the horse untended and ran to the back door of the house.

"Charley! Charley! Where are you, son? Charley, come see Daddy. Walter is here. Charley! Are you there?"

Walter ran through the house mimicking his father and calling for his brother. Christian mounted the stairs, skipping every other step as he made his way to the second floor. "Charley! Are you up here?"

Christian went through every room calling his name but found no sign of his missing son. Walter was close on his heels and shouting his brother's name at the top of his lungs. The nanny was caring for the baby and said Charley had not come home. Christian descended the stairs and went out the front door and shouted again and again for Charley without response.

Deep in despair, Christian collapsed at the kitchen table and put his head in his hands and wept. His weeping became wailing when he felt a little hand patting him on his back. "It's all right, Papa. We're going to find Charley. I promise."

Christian looked up at his hopeful son and pulled him into his lap. "Thank you, Walter. You're right. Charley will be back with us very soon." He dried his eyes and tried to be positive for Walter's sake. "What would you like for supper? I think I could make us something, but I have an even better idea. I know how much you love spaghetti and meatballs. Would you like to go to Luigi's tonight?" At that moment, Christian was regretting his decision to have dismissed his cook. He knew the meal at Luigi's would have paid her salary for at least a week, but he needed something to lift their spirits.

Walter's face brightened. "Really? Just you and me?"

"Just you and me. Go wash your face and hands then run up to your room and put on a suit. As soon as you're ready we can go. The buggy is still hitched."

Walter ran across the room to the pump located in the kitchen and then ran upstairs to change. Christian thought how fortunate they were to have such a convenience. Then before he dismissed that thought, he considered how he was going to break the news to his family that they would probably have to sell the house and move to a smaller, more modest place.

Christian ran upstairs and hurriedly changed clothes. He told the nanny he was taking Walter for dinner and to please watch out for Charley. Christian would have liked to have had time for a shower, but he knew if he paused that long, he would talk himself out of going out to eat. As he got back to the kitchen, Walter came running down the stairs.

"I'm ready Papa." Walter held his hands up for inspection. Christian looked at one side and then turned them so he could see the other side.

"You did an excellent job, young man, and you look very handsome. Let's load up and go get something to eat."

Walter ran out the back door and out to the stable. By the time Christian got to the buggy, Walter was already on the buggy bench. "Can I drive?"

"I think I can use some help. Let me get it out on the street and then I'll hand you the reins for a little bit."

Ross maneuvered the buggy out of the alley and on to East Washington Lane. There was very little traffic so he handed the reins to his son and gave him instructions to watch out for other buggies and riders and also not let the horse go too fast.

"How am I doing, Papa?"

"You're doing just fine, Walter." Walter kept the horse moving towards Luigi's Famous Italian Ristorante. It was not yet fully dark so Christian looked carefully at each buggy they passed. He also watched for anyone who was out walking. He hoped he would find another kindly neighbor leading Charley home.

When they arrived at the restaurant, an attendant helped Walter and Christian down and then took the buggy to a parking area at the rear of the building. Walter walked into the restaurant with a big smile on his face. He knew his mother and father came here periodically but he had only been there on one other occasion, and that was for his last birthday.

Luigi, who always served as maître d', warmly greeted them. "Hello again, Mr. Ross. And who is this young gentleman with you?

"Luigi, you remember Walter. He was here for his birthday supper a few months ago."

"Of course. And how are you Master Walter?" The restaurateur was dressed in an elegant black suit with a matching silk tie.

"I'm just fine, thank you." Walter motioned to his father to bend down so he could whisper in his ear. "Why did he call me Master Walter?"

Christian chuckled to himself and whispered back, "That is just a way of showing respect."

"Will Mrs. Ross be joining you this evening?

"No. She is in Atlantic City with several of our children."

"Very well. Then, gentlemen, if you will follow me, I'll lead you to your table."

Luigi led them to a table near the back corner of the dining room and held the chair for Walter. Walter beamed with delight in being treated as an important person. Christian took his seat as the maître d' placed a napkin in his lap and then did the same for Walter.

"Your waiter will be right here but would you like for me to put in an order for a bottle of your favorite Chianti?"

"Yes, thank you, Luigi. That would be lovely. And would you bring Walter a freshly squeezed lemonade?

"Certainly, sir. I'll get both of those myself." Luigi recalled

Christian always had a habit of stopping by his stand as he was leaving the restaurant and leaving a generous tip. A little extra service was always appreciated by the wealthy who were then inclined to show their appreciation in a more tangible way.

Christian knew it didn't make sense for him to spend extravagantly given his current financial position. But he knew both he and Walter needed to get their minds off the missing member of their family. He still didn't know how he was going to break the news of Charley's disappearance to his wife. He wished she was home so she could help him make decisions and so they could comfort one another. But with her recent illness, he knew it was better for her to take some time to convalesce for a while. He determined he was not going to tell her what happened, believing Charley would be back home before he had to tell her.

Luigi brought the wine and lemonade. He uncorked the wine and poured a bit in Christian's glass. Christian swirled the wine in his glass, smelled the aroma, took a sip, and then swished it in his mouth. He examined the glass, holding it so the light of the candle on the table shown through.

"This is fine. Thank you, Luigi.

The restaurant owner filled Christian's wine glass while Walter attempted to replicate the steps his father had taken. He swirled his glass of lemonade, took a sip, and held it to the candle. "This is fine, too," said Walter.

Christian and Luigi chuckled. "Very good, Master Walter. I hope you enjoy your meal tonight." With those words, Luigi slipped away and was replaced almost instantly by a waiter. He was very proper and dressed identically to Luigi. He was tall and slender and had a very thick Italian accent. Christian judged him to be at least fifty years old which would put him older than any other waiter he had seen at the restaurant. He had salt and pepper black hair and nearly snow-white sideburns.

"Good evening, gentlemen. My name is Enzo. I will be serving you this evening. I see you have already something to drink. Would you like for me to bring you menus or would you like to enjoy your drinks for a while?

"Hello, Enzo," said Christian. "I don't believe I have seen you here before."

"No, sir. I just started this week. Actually, I am Luigi's brother and partner. Until last week, I was always behind the scenes. Next year, we are planning to open a second restaurant on the other side of town."

"I certainly wish you every success in that venture. Luigi's has done very well. I know your second restaurant will be well received."

Enzo just stood at the table without further comment. Then it occurred to Christian he needed to respond about their preferences.

"Enzo, I think we are ready to order. Walter will have the spaghetti and meatballs and I'll have the Veal Marsala. And as a starter, we will share an Eggplant Stack." Christian especially enjoyed the appetizer side portion of Eggplant Parmesan served stacked and surrounded by fresh basil that had been drizzled with a balsamic reduction.

"Very good, sir." The waiter departed and Christian looked at

Walter realizing he was thoroughly enjoying his experience. As he smiled at his son, his thoughts went to Charley wondering what he was having for supper. He hoped whoever took him was treating him well.

Walter looked around the restaurant, first over one shoulder and then over the other.

"What are you looking for, Walter?"

"I wanted to see if there were any other children here." He smiled his biggest smile yet and said, "But I think I'm the only one."

Christian returned his smile but his thoughts never moved from Charley. Panic set in as he wondered about where Charley would spend the night. Absentmindedly, he drained his glass of wine. Enzo appeared and refilled his glass. Christian made a mental note to make sure that glass lasted through his dinner. He would not be any good to Walter if he got tipsy.

"Papa?"

"What is it, Walter?"

"I asked you where you thought Charley is right now?"

"I'm sorry, Walter. That's the same thing I've been wondering. I hope he's having a good meal."

"Me too, Papa. Me too."

The rest of the meal, neither Walter nor Christian had much to say. The distraction of the fancy meal had given way to the reality of their emptiness, sadness, and fear. Christian had Enzo recork the remains of the bottle of wine for him to take home. They left without dessert. Christian slipped over to Luigi and left him a generous tip, matching the one he had left for his brother.

"Mr. Ross, Master Walter. I trust your meal was good. You didn't stay long enough to have had dessert. I hope nothing was wrong with food."

"Not at all, Luigi. It was marvelous as usual. We just have some things to do at home and figured we should get started."

"Very well. I have already sent for your buggy. It should be here very soon. Please extend my well wishes to Mrs. Ross."

"I certainly will. Thanks for a wonderful meal, Luigi."

"It is my pleasure, sir. I hope you will come back soon."

When they got in their buggy, Christian took the reins and got the buggy to the road that led out to Germantown. Holding the reins toward Walter he said, "Here, Walter. Would you like to take us home?"

"I don't think so. It's no fun when I'm thinking about Charley."

Christian held the reins in his left hand and put his right arm around his son. "I know what you mean, Walter. I'm thinking about Charley too. Remember, he is going to come back safely. You promised." Christian squeezed his son to his side but Walter didn't have anything else to say.

CHAPTER 16

Thursday, July 2nd

Several hours before the sun came up, Christian was up drinking coffee. Finally around five o'clock, he heard the wagon of the Philadelphia Inquirer delivery man. He went out to the wall in front of his house and collected the newspaper. As he came back into the house, he heard the milkman at the back door collecting empty bottles and delivering their standard order of six quarts of milk and a dozen eggs. He recalled he had not changed the order as planned since several of his children were out.

Christian hurried to the back door and called after the milkman. "Excuse me, sir."

"Yes, Mr. Ross. What can I do for you?"

"My wife and most of my children are out of town for several weeks. I need to change my order to…." He paused before placing the order. The plan had been to have a standing order for two quarts of milk daily until the other children came home. But with Charley gone, he wondered for a moment if he should reduce the order further.

"Yes, sir. Change it to what?"

"I think tomorrow, I will only need two quarts of milk and we'll not need eggs but once a week. And that will be our new standard order until we let you know the other children have come home."

"I'll make that change. Would you like for me to take back the extra bottles I just left?"

In spite of his financial circumstances, he didn't think it was right to ask him to take back the milk that would surely go unused. "No, today's order is fine. Let's begin the new order tomorrow."

Christian returned to the kitchen and found the newspaper he had left on the table. He eagerly flipped through each page of the paper hoping there would be some mention of Charley, but knowing in his heart there would be no news concerning his son. He filled his coffee cup, emptying the pot for the second time that morning. He put on another pot and sat back down at the table and continued reading the newspaper.

Around six o'clock, Walter woke up and came downstairs. "Is Charley here?"

Christian sadly looked over at Walter. "No, son. He didn't come home last night. But I think he will come home today. Are you hungry? I'm just getting ready to scramble some eggs. Would you like some?"

"Yes, sir. Can I help?"

"You certainly can. Do you know how to break an egg?"

"Yes, sir. Mom taught me. She said I'm really good at it. And I don't even get shell in them—most of the time."

"That's fine. I'll get you a bowl. Now I'd like you to crack four eggs into the bowl while I build a fire in the stove."

Christian went outside to the wood stack near the back door, gathered a few split logs, and started a fire in the stove. He didn't need much heat, just enough to make their eggs. Meanwhile, Walter meticulously cracked the eggs, only having to extract one small piece of shell. He proudly presented the results to his father.

"Now take a fork and pierce each of the egg yolks like I'm doing this one. Then carefully stir them up."

"But it's mixing the white and the yellow together."

"That's what scrambled eggs are. While you're mixing them up, I'm going to put butter in the pan. Once it is melted, I'll let you cook them while I make us some toast."

Walter's face brightened. Enthusiastically he stirred the eggs under his father's supervision. "That looks just fine. Now I'll pour the eggs in the skillet. I would let you do it but you are still not quite tall enough to do it without burning yourself."

Walter closely watched his father. "All right, Walter. Now it's time for you to scramble the eggs. Use the spatula to gently stir the eggs. We must be very careful not to slouch the eggs out of the pan. And we don't want to cook them too quickly. If the pan gets too hot, we'll move it off the fire a bit and then move it back as we need to."

Christian regretted he had not had more special times with

Walter and his other children. He always told himself he was putting his family first by giving himself completely to business. The more money he made, the more opportunities it could give each of his children and the more comfortable life they would have. But all he succeeded in doing was giving all his time to making all the money he could only to lose everything. He thought if he had invested time with his children, that investment would have paid great dividends that couldn't be taken from him. Sadness enveloped him as he watched Walter master the art of cooking scrambled eggs.

Meanwhile, Christian buttered two pieces of bread, sprinkled them with a bit of sugar and cinnamon, and placed them in the oven.

"Look, Papa. I'm doing it. The eggs are cooking."

"That looks great, Walter. Let me move the skillet off the fire a bit and then I want you to scrape the pan so all of the egg gets mixed up and none of it gets over cooked. We're only going to cook it a little more. When it stops being liquid and sets up a little firmer, we are going to pull it off the stove."

Walter continued cooking the eggs until Christian pronounced them perfect. Walter sat down at the table while Christian put eggs and toast on two plates and poured them each a glass of milk. Before eating, Christian bowed his head and Walter did the same.

"Dear Lord, we're grateful for the food you've provided. We ask that you will bless it. And we ask that you will watch over Mommy and all the kids. And we especially ask that you will watch over Charley, wherever he is. A-men."

Tears dropped from Walter's eyes. He looked at his father and saw he was crying as well. They picked at their eggs and toast. It was obvious that their thoughts of Charley dampened their enthusiasm for eating the meal they had just prepared.

Christian cleared the table and washed the dishes. "Walter, I'm going to take you to Mrs. Perkins for the day, I know you like playing with Billy. I need to be out looking for Charley."

"I want to go with you, Papa."

"I can understand that but I need you to stay with Mrs. Perkins and Billy. It will probably be late when I pick you up. I need to be able to move fast today because I want to find Charley before the day is over."

"I understand, Papa. I'll be all right. Just find Charley."

Christian put down his dishcloth and bent down, picking up Walter and hugging him tightly. "You're growing up so quickly. You're too young to have to put your own feelings aside to just think about your brother. But I do appreciate you understanding."

Roy Clinton

CHAPTER 17

Christian hitched the buggy and took Walter over to Mrs. Perkins. Walter jumped down just as soon as the buggy stopped and yelled for Billy. Billy came out the door and both boys disappeared around the side of the house.

Mrs. Perkins came to the door. "Hello, Mr. Ross. Your wife told me you might be bringing the boys over for me to watch some this week. Where's Charley?"

Christian moved to the porch and took off his hat. "I'm afraid Charley's not here." Tears dripped from his eyes. "I don't know where he is."

"What? What do you mean you don't know where he is?"

Over the next several minutes, Christian told of the disappearance of both boys. He talked about the Candy Man and of finding Walter. Mrs. Perkins listened intently with her hand covering her mouth as if to guard her from the awful abduction of little Charley Ross.

"I'm headed back to the police station now. They've been searching for Charley throughout the night. Today, the search will intensify. The sergeant said he would get more manpower to conduct a proper search. I'm not sure what time I'll be back to pick up Walter."

Mrs. Perkins shook her head as she tried to ward off the horrible story she had just heard. "Mr. Ross, why don't you let Walter stay with me until Charley comes home. He and Billy get along so very well. You don't need to be worrying about him while you are searching for Charley."

"That's very kind of you, Mrs. Perkins. I know you're right but I never assumed that when I brought Walter over."

"I know you didn't. And you didn't ask. I offered. That's what neighbors are for."

"Thank you, Mrs. Perkins. Let me think about it. I'll come by this evening before it is too late to see Walter and see how he is doing. If he is all right with that arrangement, I know that will take a load off of my mind."

"Very well. You come by this evening. I think you'll find Walter to be adjusting well to the idea of spending more time with Billy."

Ross turned his buggy toward downtown and headed to the police station. When he arrived, he was surprised to find there were many buggies and horses tied out front. When he went into the station, he found uniformed policemen everywhere. He walked toward the rear of the station where he had been the day before.

Sergeant Dixon saw him walking through the station and called to him. "Mr. Ross. I'm back here. Please come join me. Can I get you a cup of coffee?"

"Yes, please. That would be nice."

"Since you're here, I take it Walter and Charley didn't come home last night. While I'm sad that's the case, it's what I anticipated. That's why all the extra policemen are here today. We're going to begin a search of the whole city. Have there been any new developments?"

"Yes, there have been. I found Walter."

"That's great! When did that happen?"

"Not long after I left here yesterday. I was on my way home and I saw a man holding his hand and walking down the road. Walter was crying. I jumped to conclusions that the man had something to do with taking the boys. As it turns out, the man was a true Good Samaritan. He had seen Walter crying and went to his aid. He told me he was trying to take Walter home."

"Why didn't you come back here and let us know? My men have been searching through the night for both of your sons and now you tell us one son has been found."

"I'm sorry, sergeant. I guess I didn't think of that."

"Well, I'm glad you found Walter. What's the name of the man who found him? I'll need his name to add to the report."

"That makes sense. He is Mr. Henry Peacock. According to him, he lives in Germantown, not far from my house."

"I'm sure it will all check out. But in cases like this, we need to follow up on every lead."

"Sergeant, have your men gathered any more leads during the

night?"

"Nothing that has led us to your son. But we have organized ourselves so that we're ready to methodically check out every part of the city. Mr. Ross, I don't mind telling you we have never had a case like this so we're also learning as we go."

"If that's supposed to make me more comfortable, it didn't work. How can I have confidence you're going to find him if you don't know what you're doing?"

"Come now, Mr. Ross. I didn't say we didn't know what we're doing. We're very skilled at all types of police work. All I'm saying is, while we have experience in finding missing persons and lost children, we simply have not had a case where a child has been abducted. Honestly, what concerns me most is why your son was taken."

"I don't know but I also don't see why that even matters."

"If we knew more about why your son was taken, we might be more likely to discover who took your son and where they have taken him."

"I'm sorry, Sergeant. I know you're doing what needs to be done. I just can't help but worry about Charley. I never dreamed he would be gone from home all night. Do you think you'll find him today?"

"I'd like to think so. What I need you to do is to be patient and let us do our work. We want to get him home just as much as you do."

"In all fairness, Sergeant. I don't think that's possible. Are you a parent?" The sergeant nodded his head. "If your son was taken, how could anyone want to find your son more than you?"

"You're right. What I should say is, as of now, the most important police case in Philadelphia is finding your son and returning him safely to you and your wife."

"Thank you, Sergeant. What do you want me to do?"

"Mr. Ross, I would like it if you would simply go home and wait for word from us that your son has been found. But if I were in your place, I know I couldn't simply go home and wait. What I think would be best is for you to join one of our search teams. We're going into each building in the city. Since we don't know where your son is, I have decided the first thing to do is to search every building in Philadelphia. That is going to be a mammoth undertaking but I believe it is the best thing to do."

"I know nothing of police work but it sounds like that makes good sense. When do we get started?"

Roy Clinton

CHAPTER 18

Thursday, July 2nd

Christian Ross was introduced to two policemen who were part of the task force charged with searching every building in Philadelphia. Webster was older than Fleming and seemed to be in charge. They climbed into a police buggy and went to their assigned section of town.

"Mr. Ross," said officer Webster, "for each building we search, I want you to stay back and let Fleming and me take the lead. My plan is to have Fleming stay on the first floor where he can monitor traffic coming and going from the building. I want you to follow me to the top floor. Then we'll split up and you and I will search every floor, room by room. Be sure to look into every box and every storage space large enough to conceal a four-year-old boy. I don't want to leave anything to chance."

"I fully agree. I have seen both of my younger boys hide in

places I didn't think big enough to hold them."

Fleming pulled the buggy to a stop in front of a four-story building. Fleming went in first followed by Webster and Ross. Fleming and Webster looked through the first floor, located the exits and did a quick count of the number of people on that floor. Then Webster took to the stairs followed by Christian. On the way Webster talked over his shoulder to Ross.

"Fleming will call the elevator car and put it out of service until we finish our search. That way the only way anyone can get out will be by the stairs. I want one of us near enough the stairs at all times so we can make sure no one slips by without us noticing."

"What do I do if I see someone going to the stairs?"

"You ask them to wait by order of the Philadelphia police and you call me immediately. No one is allowed to enter or leave the building until we finish our search."

Ross was out of breath by the time they got to the top floor. As far as he could tell, Webster was not even breathing hard. When they started climbing the stairs, Christian wondered why Webster hadn't sent the younger man. After witnessing the way he sprinted to the top of the building, he completely dismissed that thought. He was obviously very physically fit.

Webster took Ross through the first three rooms and told him how to search and how to identify potential hiding places. Ross was a quick study. Webster watched him expertly search two more rooms by himself and said he was now on his own. They cleared that floor and descended the stairs to the third story. It took no more than five minutes to completely search that floor and then to descend to the second floor.

When that was finished, they went to the first floor. There were more people and more places to hide on that floor as there were on the other floors combined. The three men split up and methodically covered every square inch of the floor. Webster knocked on the women's bathroom and got no response. He asked a nearby secretary to go in to verify it was empty. Then Fleming went in and quickly cleared it.

Without any exchange of words, Fleming moved the buggy to the next building. Ross followed Webster. While Fleming was parking the buggy Webster and Ross went in and counted people and located the exits. When Fleming appeared, Webster held up fingers indicating the number of occupants and pointed to the backdoor and then headed to the stairs.

Christian Ross literally had to run to keep up with Webster. He counted off the floors as they passed each landing—six, seven, eight. Finally, they arrived at the top floor and saw a sign announcing the eleventh floor. Ross bent double as he got to the landing. Webster was already checking the floor. By the time Ross had caught his breath, Webster was back on the stair landing signaling Ross to follow him to the floor below.

In less than fifteen minutes, the three men had cleared that building. Once again, Fleming moved the buggy and Ross followed Webster to the next building. "Mr. Ross, I hope you will not be offended by this but you're holding us up. I realize you're not in nearly as good of shape as we are. But then again, I doubt your job is as physically demanding." Ross couldn't catch his breath enough to speak so he just nodded. "I would like for you to wait in the buggy as we search the next few buildings. Your job is to look for anything that is suspicious and keep track of anyone coming or going into the buildings.

"That—that—will—be fine." Ross fought for each breath and tried not to sound as exhausted as he felt. Inwardly he was grateful he was not being expected to go into each building. As he watched the two veteran policemen continue the search, he had a new appreciation for law enforcement officers and how much of themselves they gave to their jobs. And he also felt immense gratitude for so many men giving their total focus to finding his son.

Ross moved the buggy as Webster and Fleming made their way to the next several buildings. He realized he was much better suited to driving the buggy than he was to searching buildings. For the rest of the day, he stayed in the buggy and did his best to support the policemen. When a building had three or less stories, Ross jumped out of the buggy and took his place on the search team. As evening approached, he realized they had not even taken a break to eat. He wondered how typical that was of the men he was working with and whether other policemen had the same work ethic. Christian chose to think this was the way they worked when they were dealing with an emergency.

Late in the afternoon, the search parties from across the city converged back at the central police station. Ross saw many dejected looks from men who were bone weary. Sergeant Dixon walked to the large meeting room at the back of the station. The policemen followed him and took seats behind rows of long tables. Ross marveled at the lack of idle chit-chat.

"All right men. I can tell from the lack of talking that we have not yet found Charley Ross." There was a bit of a murmur as the policemen shook their heads. "That means tomorrow is the day we find Charley." There was voiced agreement around the room.

Dixon took a large stack of papers and distributed a stack to each row of tables. "Mr. Ross brought us a photo of Charley. I've had these posters printed. Tomorrow, I want each team to take a stack of posters and hand them out as you continue your search. And I also want you to go back and take posters to each business you searched today. Every time you enter a building, I want you to place a poster at the building entrance. You can see that anyone with information about Charley's whereabouts is to report immediately to the station.

CHARLEY ROSS.

"I want each of you to get a good night's sleep and be back here in the morning at six sharp. And tomorrow, we'll work straight through until six. If you want something to eat, bring it with you. Until Charley Ross is found, we'll work twelve-hour shifts and will not take any lunch breaks. Men, I want each of you to take a poster home with you. Show it to your wife and to your neighbors. And as you look at the drawing of Charley, consider how you would feel if it was your child who was missing. Tomorrow come back and search as though you were looking for your own missing child." Dixon looked from row to row, getting eye contact with as many men as possible over about a minute.

"Dismissed. I'll see you back here in the morning."

Christian Ross wiped tears from his eyes as he listened to the impassioned speech Sergeant Dixon had given. Dixon came over to Ross and placed his big hand on his shoulder. "Mr. Ross, I'm very sorry we didn't find your son today. We'll find him. It is just a matter of time. We have never had a missing person case where we didn't find the person within a few days. And that's a record we're going to keep. I heard from Webster and Fleming that you put in a hard day with them. I'm going to suggest that you stay at home as long as you can tomorrow. I know you want to be here and you can come any time you wish. But I do hope you'll take care of your own health. While I told the men tomorrow will be the day we find Charley, you also need to be prepared for the search to drag on for several more days. It's important for you to take care of yourself."

"You're right, Sergeant. I'll do my best to get a good night's sleep and will plan on coming here in the middle of the day." Dixon extended his hand and Ross shook it and went out to his buggy. He realized he hadn't even given thought to his horse for the day. Fortunately, police stable supervisor told Mr. Ross he had taken care of his horse and would have his buggy hitched each evening for him to return home.

Roy Clinton

CHAPTER 19

As Christian Ross's buggy turned into the drive leading to the stable at Mrs. Perkins' house, Walter and Billy came out to meet him. Before Christian could climb down. Walter said, "Guess what? I get to stay with Billy until Charley comes home." He looked up to see Mrs. Perkins coming out of the house. "Isn't that right, Mrs. Perkins?"

"It sure is, Walter. That is, if it is all right with your father."

"Are you sure that is what you want to do, Walter?"

"Oh yeah. It'll be fun."

Christian looked at Mrs. Perkins who arched her eyebrows and gave a little smile that turned up only one side of her lips, as though to say, *Told you so.*

Ross smiled back. "All right. But Walter, I want you to mind Mrs. Perkins and not get into any trouble. I'll bring some extra clothes by here in the morning."

"Nonsense," said Mrs. Perkins. "Billy and Walter are the same size. I have plenty of clothes for both boys. You just give attention to finding Charley and don't worry about things here."

Christian took a deep breath and let it out. It was a relief to be able to concentrate his efforts on finding Charley, knowing Walter was being well cared for. He called after Walter to tell him good bye but he and Billy had returned to their playing.

"Thank you, Mrs. Perkins. You're a godsend. I hope this whole ordeal will be over by this time tomorrow."

"I hope so too, Mr. Ross. But for now, know Walter is in good hands." Christian climbed into his buggy and turned the horse toward home. As the buggy turned, Mrs. Perkins called out. "When you find Charley, bring him over so I can give him a big hug."

"I'll do that, Mrs. Perkins."

Ross trotted his horse back to his home. Once again, he had left every door unlocked, hoping Charley would find his way home and be waiting in the house for him.

"Charley! Charley! Are you here son?" He walked from room to room, just as he had the day before. He went to the second floor and checked out every bedroom. The nanny was rocking the baby and shook her head at Ross. Christian looked under every bed and in each chifforobe and wardrobe. Crestfallen, Christian walked back downstairs and sat down heavily at the kitchen table.

He put his head in his hands and sobbed loudly. This time he didn't have to worry about upsetting Walter. His grief was so great he didn't know how he was going to move forward. He knew he needed to eat some supper but he had no appetite. It was a comfort to him knowing that Walter was well cared for and would be eating his own supper soon.

At midnight, Christian lifted his head from the table and realized he had fallen asleep sitting in the kitchen. Mechanically, he walked out the back door to get a few pieces of wood to build a fire in the stove. He then cracked two eggs in a bowl, buttered a piece of bread, and proceeded to repeat the breakfast he had shared with Walter eighteen hours earlier.

Roy Clinton

CHAPTER 20

Friday, July 3rd

When Christian woke up the next morning, it took him a few minutes to get oriented. Initially, he had forgotten about Charley being taken. As he thought about his missing son, he remembered Walter was staying with Mrs. Perkins. While he was grateful for her generosity, he felt lonely. For the first time he could remember, he was at home with only his baby daughter and his two remaining household staff. His wife and the rest of the children were still out of town for summer vacation.

Christian knew he should get up instead of staying in bed. It looked like the sun had been up for several hours. Tears fell from his eyes. Was Charley being well cared for? What would he do if Charley was never found? Christian sat up and scolded himself for having morbid thoughts.

He dressed and walked past the empty bedrooms of his children. In the nursery, he acknowledged the nanny who was taking care of the baby. Pausing at Charley's door, he again wiped tears from his eyes. Christian proceeded downstairs and walked through the kitchen to the backdoor. He retrieved the two quarts of milk that were left earlier that morning. He quickly scrambled two of the remaining eggs as he thought of Walter and how they had cooked breakfast together the day before.

When he finished eating, he thought he would go get the newspaper and drink a pot of coffee as he read it. Walking out the front door, he noticed a piece of paper tied to a rock. He quickly looked at it but it didn't make sense to him. The handwriting looked like that of a child. He dropped the rock and placed the note in his pocket and continued walking out to the front wall to collect the newspaper.

He put on the coffee and took a seat at the kitchen table to read. As he started reading the newspaper, he recalled picking up the note. He retrieved it from his pocket and laboriously read.

Mr. Ross- be not uneasy you son charly bruster he al writ we as got him and no powers on earth can deliver out of our hand. You wil hav two pay us befor you git him from us. an pay us a big cent to. if you put the cops hunting for him yu is only defeeting yu own end. we is got him fitt so no living power can gits him from us a live. if any aproch is maid to his hidin place that is the signil for his instant anihilation. if yu regard his lif puts no one to search for him you money can fech him out alive an no other existin powers don't deceve yuself and think the detectives can git him from us for that is one imposebel yu here from us in few day.

He couldn't believe what he was reading. Christian read it again to make sure he had the message straight. Any fantasies he entertained about Charley being home by evening immediately evaporated.

Christian ran out the back door to the stable. Hurriedly, he hitched the horse to the buggy, laid the whip to the horse's rump and raced to the police station. He continually whipped his horse all the way to the station. When he arrived, he jumped from the buggy and ran inside, not even seeing the police stableman who attempted to greet him.

Ross ran to the back of the police station yelling as he went. "Sergeant Dixon! Sergeant Dixon!"

Dixon walked out of his office and saw Christian running toward him with a paper in his hand. "Sergeant! I have a letter from the men who took Charley!"

The sergeant ushered Ross into his office and was joined by Detective Ramsey. Christian handed the letter to Dixon who read it, while Ramsey read it over his shoulder.

"Well, this changes things," said Ramsey.

"It certainly does," said Dixon.

Christian looked confused. "I don't understand. How does that change things?"

"Well for one thing," replied Ramsey, "we know the motive for your son being taken. The men are after money. We had assumed that might be the case but we didn't have any confirmation until now. That means you will likely receive another letter with their specific demand. All they said here is you will have to pay them a 'big cent.' The next letter will tell you what that means."

"Is that what happens in cases like this?" asked Christian.

Ramsey had a sardonic smile on his face. "That's just it, Mr. Ross. There has never been a case like this. While my most immediate concern is for the return of your son, I'm also concerned with the fact that others will follow suit and try to get money by taking children."

"I don't care what they ask for, I'll pay it. I'll pay any amount to get my son back."

"I know that's how you feel," Ramsey said. "But beyond setting a precedent for other criminals to follow if you pay, I'm guessing the men will find out how easy it is to get money from you and demand more."

Christian stood and leaned across the desk. "Then what am I supposed to do? I can't just ignore their demand. They have said they will kill Charley." Ross's eyes filled with tears that dripped onto the desk.

"We'll have to figure out the next step," said the detective. "What I'm thinking right now is that we need to enlist the help of the public in a big way. Sergeant, how do you feel about putting advertisements in the major newspapers? We could put the poster of Charley in the paper, and, if you're willing, Mr. Ross, you could offer a reward for his safe return."

"I think that is a grand idea," said Dixon. "Even though the note said don't tell the police, they must be aware by now the police are involved. Mr. Ross, if you are willing to pay the expense of the advertisements, I'll write them up and get them out to the newspapers. We can start with the Philadelphia Inquirer and the New York Times. I would like for those newspapers to suggest others that should carry the ads."

"Of course, I'll pay for them. Whatever is needed. If I have to sell everything I have, I'll do it. I have to get Charley back."

"Don't fret, Mr. Ross," said Detective Ramsey. "The positive thing about the letter is that we can assume Charley is alive and well at this moment. It's in the best interest of those who have taken him to make sure he remains in good health. He's their ticket to getting paid."

"So, what do we do now?" asked Ross.

"Besides continuing our search and enlisting the public's help through the newspapers, we wait. The men will be making another demand soon. They will tell you how much money they want and how they want you to pay them."

"So, then I just pay them?"

"We'll cross that bridge when we come to it," said Ramsey. "Right now, I'm thinking we'll first demand some way for them to be able to prove Charley's alive and in good health."

"I wish you would stop talking about Charley and questioning whether he is alive. I hadn't even thought of any other possibility until today."

"I'm sorry, Mr. Ross," said the detective. "You wanted to be close to our investigation. We must consider every possible circumstance." His voice got a pronounced edge on it as he continued, "And if you're not able to let us do our job, I'm going to ask that you stay away from here completely and let us do our work."

"I'm sorry, Detective. I didn't mean any disrespect. You do your job the way you need to. I'll stay out of the way. Please let me continue to stay here and keep up with the investigation."

"So long as you don't impede our progress," said Ramsey, "you can stay. That is, as far as I'm concerned. Sergeant Dixon has the final say."

"Yes, you can stay," said Dixon. "But Mr. Ross, please remember we're all on the same side and we're doing everything in our power to get your son back—and get him back alive and healthy."

Christian nodded as he once again wiped his eyes. He sat back down and folded his hands in his lap. "You'll not even know I'm around. I'll stay out of the way. Gentlemen, thank you for being so committed to finding my son."

"We're all fathers," said Ramsey. "We'll search for him as though we were searching for our own sons."

Ross nodded his thanks as Dixon and Ramsey continued the conversation about how to continue the investigation.

Roy Clinton

CHAPTER 21

Over the next three weeks, several letters were received from the kidnappers. The second letter was received on Tuesday, July seventh. It demanded a ransom of twenty thousand dollars be paid for the return of Charley. While Christian Ross didn't have the money, a wealthy friend stepped forward and offered to pay the ransom.

The police, fearing such a payment would only encourage similar kidnappings, persuaded Ross not to pay the ransom. The authorities were united in their belief Charley would not be harmed by refusing to pay the kidnappers. They told Christian when he refused to pay the ransom the kidnappers would eventually give up and leave Charley on a street where he would eventually find his way home. It was their opinion the kidnapping was just a drunken frolic that got out of hand.

More letters were received making additional demands. Most of these were mailed from various places around Philadelphia, but the letters also stated that Charley was not being held in Philadelphia. In all, there were two dozen letters received. Some of them were mailed from New York City, the Hudson Valley, and as far away as New Brunswick.

The public was greatly moved by the story of Charley Ross's disappearance. Searches were mobilized from Trenton to Baltimore. Coal yards, outhouses, swamps, and forests were searched. The whole country was focused on the unfolding saga of the kidnapping of Charles Brewster Ross.

CHAPTER 22

Saturday, July 25th

John Crudder arrived in Philadelphia on Saturday afternoon armed with a letter of introduction from the President.

To Whom It May Concern:

Mr. John Crudder is Special Agent to the President of the United States of America. He is empowered to conduct investigations on my behalf and answers only to me. All law enforcement agencies, as well as other organizations and citizens, are directed to provide him all cooperation and resources as are necessary for his investigations.

Ulysses S. Grant
President of the United States

He hired a horse and buggy and went immediately to the central police station. After inquiring as to the person who was in charge of the Charley Ross case, he was led back to Sergeant Dixon's office. He knocked on the frame of the open door.

"Good afternoon, Sergeant. My name is John Crudder."

The sergeant raised his eyes from the papers he was studying on his desk and looked at John. He couldn't help but smile at the sight of the small man standing in the doorway with his hat in his hand. Dixon pushed back from his desk. "And how can I help you, Mr. Crudder?"

"Actually, I was hoping I could be of service to you. I used to be the marshal in Bandera, Texas, and I'm a pretty good investigator."

Dixon smiled. "Is that so? Well I'm proud for you. I'm not sure where Bandera is but I do know that Philadelphia is not some backwater town in Texas. I appreciate your offer but I think we have all of the help we need." Dixon returned his attention to the papers on his desk. John stepped forward unfolding the letter from the President as he did so. He laid the letter in front of the sergeant and stepped back.

As Dixon read the letter, his mouth dropped open. When he looked up, John pulled his badge from his pocket and opened the wallet so the sergeant could read his identification card. Dixon stood and extended his hand to Crudder as the shock registered on his face. "I'm sorry, Mr. Crudder, if I seemed impertinent. I didn't know—I mean—I have never seen a letter—I've— Mr. Crudder, you're indeed welcome here. I would be most pleased to accept your offer of help. You must certainly be an outstanding investigator for the President to send you here."

John reflected on the great change in the sergeant's attitude when he realized he was there at the behest of the President. "Thank you, Sergeant. If I'm not interrupting too much, I wonder if you could bring me up to date on the investigation?"

"No, sir. You're not interrupting at all. I welcome your help."

For the next half of an hour, Dixon brought John Crudder up to speed with the investigation. Detective Ramsey came into the office and was introduced to John by Dixon. In order to cut off any further debate, he shook Ramsey's hand and held up his badge case with the other. Ramsey registered the same initial shock as Dixon. Neither man had ever heard of the President having a special agent.

All initial defensiveness disappeared as Ramsey added information about the investigation and both men responded openly to Crudder's questions. John asked about any outside investigation that may also be taking place.

"There's a private investigator," said Ramsey. "His name is Arthur Boseman. I didn't see why he was needed but Mr. Ross said he agreed to employ him to give us extra help." Ramsey and Dixon glanced at each other as Ramsey continued, "Frankly, he's a pain in the...well, let me just say he's a pain. So far, all he has done is muddy things up for us."

"What caused Mr. Ross to hire him? It sounds like he's been pleased with the work you have been doing and having been allowed to be kept close to the investigation."

"That's what I don't fully understand," said Ramsey. "Mr. Ross just brought him to the station one morning and said he had hired him to help with the investigation. He said he was sure Boseman could provide some insights the police had missed. It was pointless to try to talk him out of his decision—especially with Boseman standing there. Later we were able to talk to Mr. Ross alone but he was adamant that Boseman was going to stay on the case."

"How has he been involved?"

"So far, he's just been asking questions," said Dixon. "We can't see any investigation that he's been doing. He's most interested in any suspicions we have about who the kidnappers are and who might be sending the letters from multiple places."

John thought it curious Boseman seemed to only be trying to pry information out of the police rather than adding to the investigative efforts. Crudder was not sure how the suggestion he was going to make would be received but he plowed ahead anyway.

"Gentlemen, I'm going to give some attention to finding out more about Mr. Boseman. Meanwhile, I have a suggestion that you may not readily accept—especially given Boseman's intrusion. I want to hire the Pinkerton Agency out of Chicago to help us."

Ramsey stood and shook his head. "With all due respect, Mr. Crudder, I don't see how it will help bringing in an outside agency. In fact, I completely oppose the move."

Crudder was prepared for the opposition. "Recently, I used Pinkertons for a personal matter in New York City and found them not only to be excellent investigators but also skilled at working in concert with the police. In addition to that, the Department of

Justice has contracted with Pinkertons to be their investigative arm for bringing in those guilty of violating federal law. While kidnapping is not a federal offence—and I'm not sure why it's not—I'll see that all expenses involving their work will be paid."

Ramsey thought about what Crudder had said. "I didn't realize they were doing work for the Department of Justice."

"My thought in bringing them in is to add manpower and other resources to the investigation. However, I think it is important that there only be one central command. And that remains with the Philadelphia Police Department. The two of you will coordinate all parts of the investigation and they will report to you. Think of them as an extension of your department. And please, gentlemen, make use of their expertise. I'm bringing them in because of their investigating expertise. Be open to them pursuing leads they surface. My hope is they will help shorten the time it takes to recover Charley Ross alive."

Ramsey and Dixon nodded their heads. "I agree with that," said Ramsey. "Mr. Crudder, thank you for your confidence in our department. And thanks for seeing the need for them to be a part of our investigation and not pulling in a different direction."

"Now if you can recommend a good hotel for me and tell me how to find Mr. Boseman, I'll not take any more of your time. I'll be checking in with you regularly to get an update on the investigation."

After receiving the information he requested, the Midnight Marauder excused himself. On his way to the hotel, John stopped at the telegraph office and sent a telegram to Chicago.

Mr. Allen Pinkerton
Pinkerton National Detective Agency
Chicago, Illinois

Re: Charley Ross Kidnapping. Send ten of your best detectives to Philadelphia Police Department. Report to Sergeant Dixon. Supply any additional manpower he needs. Bill me care of Howard Hastings, 5ᵗʰ Avenue, NYC.

John Crudder
Philadelphia, Pennsylvania

CHAPTER 23

Sunday, July 26th

John Crudder slept well in his hotel. He found out the Morris House was built in 1787 and was only two blocks from Independence Hall. When he came down for breakfast, he asked that his buggy be hitched and ready to depart when he finished his meal. He also asked for directions to the Germantown neighborhood.

Crudder arrived at the home of Christian Ross shortly after eight o'clock and knocked on the door. He was surprised when Mr. Ross himself answered the door. Crudder introduced himself and showed Ross his badge. He was ushered into the large parlor and invited to sit down.

"May I offer you some coffee, Mr. Crudder? I just put on a fresh pot." John found it interesting that Ross said he had made the coffee. He wondered where the household staff was.

"Yes, that would be nice, thank you."

"Cream and sugar?"

"No, thank you. Black will be just fine." Crudder looked around the parlor and realized there was a layer of dust over all the hard surfaces. He also recalled seeing the yard was overgrown and untended. He stood and followed Ross to the kitchen. "Do you mind if I join you in here? It'll make it easier for me to take notes if I can do it at the table."

"Of course. Sit where you'd like while I get the coffee." Crudder noticed dirty dishes in the sink and a dirty skillet on the stove. The trash can in the corner of the room was overflowing with garbage. It was obvious there were no household staff around.

Ross served the coffee and took a seat beside Crudder. "So how may I be of service, Mr. Crudder?"

"Please call me John. May I call you Christian?"

"Certainly, sir." Ross seemed uneasy to Crudder. "I must say I'm surprised the President would be interested in the disappearance of Charley."

"It is more than a disappearance, Christian. Charley has been kidnapped."

"Quite right. That's what I meant to say. It's just hard to get used to saying that. I liked it better when I could tell myself Charley was just away and would be back soon. Even though I knew men had taken him, I hoped they would just tire of taking care of a child and return him. But after they asked for money, I knew he wasn't coming home soon."

Crudder questioned Mr. Ross about the details of the case. He covered the facts as related to him by the police and asked if they were correct. Then he proceeded to ask more detailed questions about the Ross family, the location of his wife and other children, his work, finally coming to his financial health.

"I was surprised when you answered your front door. I was expecting a butler." Ross's eyes moved furtively, replying, "Oh, the butler is on vacation. I think he went to see relatives in New York."

John nodded, "I see. How about the housekeeper and cook? Are they also on vacation?"

Ross cleared his throat. "Actually, I gave them some time off since I wouldn't be needing them while my wife was out of town."

Crudder continued watching as Ross grew increasingly more uncomfortable. "How long have you been having financial problems?"

"What are you talking about? I don't have any financial problems."

"Mr. Ross, I can't help you if you continue to lie to me. Tell me about your financial problems."

Ross whimpered and bent his head down to the table. When he raised it, he was crying.

"I'm broke. I got completely wiped out by the stock market crash last year. Nobody knows about it except for my wife. You can't tell anyone. I'll be ruined in this town."

"So, you're keeping up the fiction for your friends and neighbors that there has been no change in your financial condition?"

"That's right. Appearances are everything. My business is

doing fairly well. There's always a demand for dry goods. But my living expenses have been so great I've not been able to continue life as it had been." He paused and wiped his eyes. "My neighbors just think I was being a bit eccentric when I let go of the landscape staff. I told them I was trying to teach my children the value of work by getting them to help out with yard work. And we have not let any neighbors into the house since I let the maids go. I didn't want them to see how we're living. As far as they know, things are just as they have always been. I had assumed some of my neighbors and associates also had all their assets in the stock market and were in the same financial mess but it looks like I'm the only one I know of who has been impacted by it."

Crudder listened as Ross explained the dire circumstances and the façade he kept up. Ross told about how a friend had offered to pay the ransom but how he rebuffed the offer. He told the friend it was not needed, but the friend insisted saying that would give him a feeling of having a part in finding Charley.

"I reluctantly agreed to accept his offer but the police were completely opposed to paying the ransom. They said there was no guarantee Charley would be returned and they were afraid the kidnappers would continue to demand more money from me."

"I've had some personal experience with kidnapping. While none of us yet know how things will turn out, I tend to agree with the police. I think we stand a better chance of finding Charley if we put our efforts into investigation." Ross nodded his head in agreement.

"That brings me to Mr. Boseman. With your current financial

problems, how it is you were able to afford to hire a private investigator?"

Ross's demeanor changed and he was, at once, fully involved in the conversation. "That was a great stroke of luck on my part. Mr. Boseman came to the house a couple of days ago and said he had great experience in finding missing and lost children. He said he would stop at nothing to find Charley. I told him I was not in a position to pay for a private investigator but he said he would only charge me a dollar a day. Imagine that. I have an expert willing to help me and only charge me a dollar a day."

"Yeah, imagine that," said Crudder. John asked additional questions until he felt he had all the information he needed. There were many more questions about Christian's business dealings and his work associates. After exposing Ross's duplicity concerning his financial condition, Crudder judged he was being transparent with his answers to other questions. Lastly, John got Boseman's address from Christian and excused himself.

CHAPTER 24

Monday, July 27th

Crudder spent the rest of Sunday watching Boseman from afar. He was a huge man with hands so large that they didn't seem to fit his frame. Crudder could tell from his musculature that Boseman was used to hard work. He also guessed Boseman was handy with his fists, since private investigators may be faced with frequent occasions where physical prowess is called for.

John watched Boseman leave his house in his buggy in the middle of the afternoon. He followed Boseman from a distance, curious as to where he was going. Boseman drove to the other side of Philadelphia. Along the way, he continued to look around to see if anyone was following or paying any attention to him. Crudder remained a full quarter mile behind Boseman and, as far as he could tell, didn't do anything to attract Boseman's attention.

After about an hour's ride, Boseman arrived at a mailbox located at a busy intersection. He looked both ways to see if he was being observed. Not seeing anyone paying him any mind, Boseman climbed down and dropped a letter into the mailbox.

John wished he could have known to whom he wrote and what he said. He recalled hearing the policemen saying letters from the kidnappers had been received from all around Philadelphia. Crudder felt certain he was observing someone intimately involved in the kidnapping.

Boseman returned to his buggy and again looked around to see if anyone was watching him. He then drove back to his home with Crudder following at a distance. The drive gave John time to start putting together the pieces of the investigation.

He watched Boseman's home until late in the evening but didn't see any other suspicious activity. However, he had plenty of suspicions about Boseman. Why would a private investigator agree to work for a dollar a day? While that was decent wage for many jobs, Crudder knew competent private investigators commanded a significantly greater fee.

He was also suspicious that Boseman's contact with the police was limited to gathering information about their investigation. He was more concerned with finding out what the police were doing than he was with finding Charley. Crudder was long on suspicion and short on proof that Boseman had any nefarious purpose. He decided to follow his suspicions as far as they would go.

Monday morning around eight thirty, Crudder observed Boseman behind his house hitching his buggy. John drove down the alley and parked his buggy right in front of Boseman's, effectively blocking him.

"Mr. Boseman," said Crudder as he descended from his buggy. "Are you Mr. Arthur Boseman?"

"What if I am, shorty?"

"I need to ask you some questions."

"And I need you to move your buggy," said Boseman as he climbed into his buggy. "I've got an appointment and you're in my way."

"I'm sorry, Mr. Boseman, but I must insist you come down. I'm a federal officer. Let's go into your house where we can talk privately."

"Oh, I'm coming down all right but I'm not answering any of your questions." Boseman jumped from his buggy in the direction of Crudder and took a wild swing. John stepped to the side and landed a punch in the big man's face and then unloaded two more into his stomach. Boseman shook himself but remained on his feet. He turned and renewed his attack on John. This time he faked with his right fist. When John moved out of the way, Boseman matched his move and let go with a powerful left into Crudder's midsection.

Crudder was stunned by the power behind the punch and fell to the ground. As he tried to get up, Boseman kicked John in the ribs. John went back down on the ground and knew if he didn't do something soon, the big man would badly hurt him, or worse.

John rolled several times to get out of the way of Boseman but the mountain of a man ran after him and landed two more ferocious kicks into John's ribs. Boseman moved in close to finish John off and raised his foot to crush John's skull. John lay still until Boseman's foot was fully cocked and then reached up, grabbed the foot and twisted it as he got to his feet.

As Boseman went down, John wished he could rest for a moment and try to catch his breath. But he knew if he delayed, Boseman would regain the advantage. John had no doubt Boseman would kill him if he got the chance.

John unleashed a powerful kick into Boseman's face and then did it again. As Boseman was writhing in pain, John kicked him three times in quick succession in the ribs. Boseman rolled away from John and started getting to his feet. As he was standing, John met him with a mighty uppercut into the jaw. Boseman's eyes lost focus and he fell backward beside his buggy. John was sure he had knocked the big man unconscious.

As he considered his next move, a plan quickly formed. John took a length of rope from the buggy and tied Boseman's hands behind his back. He was careful to make the bonds tight but he also was sure, given time, Boseman would be able to work himself free. John tied the man's feet and then went to the corner of the stable and got a bucket of water that he threw in Boseman's face.

The big man regained his senses and coughed from the water that had filled his mouth. After a moment, Boseman realized he was tied up. "Hey, what are you doing? I'm going to get loose and kill you, mister."

"I don't think you're going to kill anyone. I'm going to help you up so we can go into the house. If you try anything, I'll see if I can teach you another lesson." John bent down and helped the big man to his feet. "Now hop into your house. I have some questions I need to ask."

"I'm not hopping anywhere. Now untie me and get out of here."

Crudder gave Boseman a hard push and the big man fell back and hit the ground hard. "I'm going to help you get to your feet again. Are you ready?" Crudder took Boseman by the arm and helped him up. "This time you're going to hop into your house. Or would you like for me to persuade you some more?"

"I'll go. Just quit pushing me around."

Crudder took his arm and provided direction as Boseman provided the momentum. Boseman made it up the steps and onto the porch. John pushed open the backdoor and guided Boseman inside. Once they got into the living room, John gave him a shove so Boseman landed roughly on the floor.

"Why'd you do that? I did what you said. I hopped. Will you quit pushing me around?"

"Mr. Boseman, I'm afraid you're in trouble. My name is John Crudder and I work for the federal government."

"I haven't done anything," Boseman protested. "You don't have anything on me. I'm a law-abiding citizen."

"That's hardly the case, Mr. Boseman. We know you're involved in kidnapping Charley Ross." Boseman's face registered his shock. If Crudder had any doubts to his involvement prior to that, those doubts disappeared when he saw the recognition on Boseman's face. "And if you are not the mastermind of the operation, you know who is. Actually, I think you're the one who planned it."

"You don't know what you're talking about. I haven't done anything with Charley Ross. I'm a private investigator who's been hired by Christian Ross to find his son. You can check with the police. They'll tell you. I'm helping them. Check it out. You'll see."

"Oh, I know you're a private investigator. But we also know you've been mailing the ransom letters to Mr. Ross. And we know the only thing you're doing with the investigation is finding out how much the police know so you can try to stay ahead of them. But you've been caught. I'm going to see that you're prosecuted. Mr. Boseman, you're going to jail for a long time."

The big man pulled against his bonds and yelled at Crudder. "I don't know who you think you are. I'm going to kill you. You can't treat me like this. Let me loose, right now."

"Mister Boseman, I'm going to get you up into a chair. I need to make sure you are tied up tightly because I'm going to get the police so they can take you to jail. Now roll to the side so I can help you up. And remember what I've already done to you. If you try anything, you'll be going down again."

Crudder helped Boseman into a chair and then got another length of rope and tied him to the chair. He was careful to tie him tightly although he felt Boseman would have no trouble getting loose. When he finished making a big production out of tying him up and then testing to make sure the ropes were tight, Crudder took a deep breath.

"I'll be back in less than an hour. You should be fine here until then. Don't try to get away. I've tied the ropes so they will only get tighter if you try to escape. Do you care to make a confession before I leave?"

"Mister," Boseman said, "you don't have any idea what you've stumbled into. You're going to regret you ever heard of Charley Ross."

Roy Clinton

CHAPTER 25

John just smiled and walked out the door. He mounted his buggy and drove out of the alley and out onto the street. If Boseman did as he hoped, it would only be a few minutes before he broke free and led him to others involved in the kidnapping.

Crudder guided his buggy off the street where he still had an unobstructed view of Boseman's buggy. He didn't have to wait long until Boseman burst out of the door, got into his buggy, and rode rapidly down the street. John held back to make sure Boseman wouldn't see him. When Boseman was nearly out of sight, John pulled his buggy onto the road and followed him.

About thirty minutes later, John watched as Boseman pulled his buggy into the train station. Crudder saw him go to the ticket window and then run to catch one of the trains. After Boseman was onboard, John went to the same ticket window and showed his badge briefly to the agent on duty and then returned the badge holder to his pocket.

"Excuse me, ma'am. Where was the man going who just bought a ticket?"

"I'm sorry, sir, but I can't give out that kind of information."

John read the name tag on the ticket agent. "Mrs. Woolford, I appreciate your professionalism. But if you don't answer my question, you can be charged with obstructing a federal investigation. Is that what you want?"

The woman's mouth turned sad and her eyes began to get misty. "I'm sorry, mister. I didn't mean any harm. I'm just trying to do my job as best I can."

"I understand, Mrs. Woolford. Now where is that man going?"

"He bought a first-class ticket to the end of the line. He's headed for New York City."

"Thank you, Mrs. Woolford. Now I would like to purchase a ticket to New York City. I would like a seat in the car behind that man."

"Yes sir. Whatever you say. That car is also first class. Will that be all right with you?" Before waiting for an answer, she continued, "Am I in trouble? I've never been in trouble before."

"No ma'am. You're not in trouble. But the next time a federal officer asks you questions, you might want to consider answering."

"Yes, sir. I'll do that."

John turned back to the ticket agent and pulled a paper from his pocket. "Please have someone take care of my horse and buggy. This paper has the address of the agency that rented the buggy.

Here is enough money to pay for the rental and five dollars extra for any person you can get to go tell them where to find their horse and buggy. And here is an additional five dollars for you, Mrs. Woolford, for your trouble."

Her eyes grew large as she looked at the fistful of cash she held. "Thank you, sir. My son is coming by in a little while to eat breakfast with me. Will it be all right if I wait and get him to care for your rental buggy?"

"Yes, that'll be fine." John tipped his hat and said, "Thank you for your assistance."

John took his ticket and boarded the train. Instead of going directly to his seat, he went to the car where Boseman was seated to verify he was there. Boseman was in his assigned seat and was staring out the window. Crudder knew the dining car was toward the front of the train so there should not be any reason for Boseman to come back to his car.

Crudder wished he had eaten breakfast before he started following Boseman. He knew he wouldn't get anything to eat on the train. But that was a small sacrifice if he was able to get a break in the case by following Boseman.

The trip to New York City lasted only three hours. Before the train pulled into the station, John got up and walked to the platform between the cars so he could observe Boseman. The big man got up and walked forward to get ready to exit the train. When the train stopped, Boseman was the first person off. As other passengers disembarked, John got off and pulled his hat down low on his forehead to hide his face.

Boseman didn't look around but went immediately to a stable near the station. He paid the fare and climbed up onto the buggy seat and popped the whip for the horse to hear. It was obvious wherever Boseman was going, he was in a hurry.

John watched Boseman leave and hurried to the stable. He quickly hired another buggy and set out after the suspected outlaw. Initially, Crudder was afraid Boseman had slipped away but after a few blocks he saw Boseman's buggy. He followed from a discrete distance. After several minutes, he realized Boseman was headed for the ferry crossing into Brooklyn. John slowed his buggy and tried to determine his next move. If he got on the ferry with Boseman, he was sure Boseman would recognize him. But if he waited for the next ferry, Boseman would get away.

The only thing Crudder could do was to take the same ferry and hope Boseman didn't notice him. He knew there was a risk but it couldn't be helped. Crudder pulled his hat down low on his forehead. John paid the fare for the ferry and was guided on so he was directly behind Boseman.

As the ferry left the dock, John risked looking up to see what Boseman was doing. He was oblivious to being followed. John didn't take any chances and again lowered his head and didn't move from that position until the boat docked.

John followed Boseman into the Brooklyn Heights neighborhood. After a while, he pulled the buggy in front of a house on Hicks Street. Crudder stopped his buggy well short of the home, climbed down, and walked between the houses and saw there was an alley that connected all the houses on that block. He went down to the house where Hicks ended. Crudder was aware of the risk in snooping around in the daylight but he had no choice if he was going to find out what really happened to Charley Ross.

When he got to the house where Boseman parked his buggy, Crudder nonchalantly walked to the back porch. When he got closer, he heard Boseman speaking to another man. John went to the corner of the porch so he would not be in the line of sight if the men looked his way.

"I told you never to come here. What were you thinking?" The voice was gruff and hushed.

"I didn't have any choice. A federal officer came to my house. He knew all about my part in the kidnapping. Just look at me. He beat me to within an inch of my life."

"What did you tell him?"

"Listen, Hopper," Boseman protested, "I didn't tell him anything. But he tied me up and went to get the police to arrest me."

"You're an idiot. No one knew about me. You probably led the police to me."

"That's not true. Nobody followed me. I'm smart enough not to let that happen."

"Like I said, you're an idiot. No one was to have contact with me here—ever."

"But you met Mosher here. You hired him to do the kidnapping."

"You know what I mean. No one else knew about me and no one else knew where I lived but you," said Hopper.

"I just wanted you to know that the law is on to us. We've got to be careful. I can never go back to Philadelphia again. My old life is over."

"Just settle down. There's no need to panic. We're doing just fine."

"You don't know what you're talking about. I've got to get away. I don't know what to do. Where do I go?" asked Boseman.

"I would suggest you head south. Get as far away from Philadelphia as possible and start a new life there."

"How am I supposed to do that? I only had enough money for a train ticket to get here."

"What did you do with your money? I gave you a thousand dollars for expenses."

"It's in my house."

"You idiot. Why'd you leave it there?"

"Quit calling me that," said Boseman. "I'm not an idiot. I just didn't think about the money when I was escaping. All that mattered to me was getting away before that federal officer had me arrested."

"There is something that doesn't make sense about that federal officer. Why didn't he just take you in?"

"How am I supposed to know? All I know is he beat me and then tied me up. He said he was sending the police to arrest me."

Hopper considered Boseman's words. "Either he was not a federal officer at all and was there just to get information from you, or he wanted you to escape so he could follow you here."

"Believe me, Hopper. He didn't follow me. He couldn't have. I would have seen him. Nobody followed me."

Hopper was silent as he listened to Boseman. He had to deal with him before he became a greater liability. How could he get rid of him without calling more attention to himself?

"You've got to give me more money. I have to get away."

"Where do you expect me to get more money? The parents haven't paid us yet. If you had done a better job on the letters, we wouldn't be having this conversation. I don't know how I got mixed up with you in the first place."

"You're getting twenty thousand in ransom. I want part of that."

"I've already promised Mosher half of that to pay his crew."

"What? You're going to give him half the money?

Harrison Hopper just smiled. It was obvious to Boseman, Hopper wasn't planning on paying Mosher, even though he was the one who took the risk and kidnapped the boy. *If he'll double cross Mosher, I wonder if he will do the same to me?* Boseman knew the answer to his question before he finished his thought. He knew he was at risk. It was a mistake to have come to New York. He should have just run as far from Philadelphia as he could get.

"I tell you what I'll do," said Hopper. "I don't have any money here but I can get it. I'll go ahead and pay you your share and then you clear out. However, instead of five thousand, I'll get you three thousand. I think that's fair since you didn't complete the job."

Boseman brightened. "That'll be fine. With three thousand dollars, I can go south and get a new start. When can you get it?"

"I'll go to the bank in just a little while and meet you tonight. But I don't want you to come back to my house."

"You just name the place and I'll be there." Boseman was already spending the money in his imagination.

"I'll meet you tonight at ten o'clock. Go to the construction site where they're building the new bridge. You can't miss it. There is a huge foundation for the bridge support and it is about half built. I'll be waiting for you on the side closest to the water. Make sure you're on time. I can't hang around there long." Hopper paused and then added, "And Boseman, don't park a buggy near the bridge. Get out of your buggy and walk there so you will not attract any attention."

Crudder had heard enough. While he didn't know the location of Charley Ross, he did know who was behind the kidnapping. He slipped away from the house and back to the alley. Casually, he walked back to his buggy, giving Boseman time to get out of sight.

When John emerged from between the houses, he saw Boseman driving off. There was a smile on his face as he contemplated his new life with three thousand dollars. Crudder had not been able to see either man's face during their conversation but he was still certain Hopper had no intention of paying Boseman any more money. To Hopper, Boseman was expendable. The more loose ends eliminated, the less risk and more money for Hopper.

CHAPTER 26

Shortly after eight, Crudder had selected a hiding place and was waiting for Hopper and Boseman to come to their meeting. From his vantage point, he felt he was able to see both men but not be seen by them.

Crudder had been in place for less than an hour when Hopper slipped into the shadows of the construction site. John wasn't sure if Hopper was preparing to ambush Boseman or if he was wanting to ward off an attack by Boseman. One thing was for certain. There would be a violent confrontation in just over an hour.

A few minutes after ten, Boseman walked into the construction site. In a loud whisper, he called out.

"Hopper. Are you there?" After several seconds, he called out louder. "Hopper. Where are you?"

"Psst," came the response from Hopper. "Come over here. Did anybody follow you?"

"Of course not. I was careful. Where are you? It's hard to see. I'll strike a match."

"No! Don't do that. Someone might see it. Come over here.

There's enough light for you to be able to count your money."

Boseman pressed ahead in the dark. Crudder slipped from his hiding place and moved toward the two men. The light was so dim, he couldn't see his own feet. There was a noise that sounded like someone dropping a bag to the ground. Crudder listened but neither man was talking. He couldn't make out anything in the dark.

John waited two full minutes when he heard a horse whinny and a buggy moving on the road leaving the construction site. John pulled his gun and ran toward the last place he had heard voices. He struck a match and found Boseman lying in a pool of blood but there was no sign of Hopper.

Crudder swore under his breath. He had intended to eavesdrop and find out more about the kidnapping but also prevent any violence from taking place. He had not accomplished either.

John was certain Hopper was headed back to his home. Wasting no time, John ran to his buggy and got the horse to gallop toward Hopper's home. He stopped at the end of the alley and slipped up to the porch where he had overheard the conversation earlier that day. John could hear Hopper moving around inside.

Believing time was critical, John slipped into the unlocked back door and made his way toward light that was coming from a bedroom. He could hear Hopper humming to himself. John thought Hopper must be pleased with himself. John crept toward the bedroom as Hopper's humming got louder. When he finally got to the door, he saw Hopper had his back to him and was getting ready for bed. Hopper was just shy of six feet tall, clean shaven, and had almost snow-white hair. John guessed he was about sixty years old.

Hopper had slipped out of his shirt and trousers and was putting on a night shirt. John waited to make his move until Hopper had the nightshirt over his head and was trying to thread his arms into place.

Crudder stepped into the room. "Mr. Hopper, I want you to keep your hands right where they are. Don't move unless you're ready to die."

Hopper froze in place. "Can I at least get my head free? I can't see a thing."

"Do it, but don't drop your arms if you value your life."

Hopper worked his head through the opening of his nightshirt and looked at John. Slowly a smile crossed his face. "Now I'm guessing you're that so-called federal agent Boseman told me about. Well, sonny, you don't look like much of a threat to me."

He started to lower his arms when John pulled one of the daggers from his back scabbard and let it fly. It landed precisely where John was aiming and struck deep in his shoulder.

"Aaahhh!" Hopper writhed in pain and grabbed his wounded shoulder in an attempt to minimize the pain. "What'd you do that for? You ruined my shoulder."

"I told you not to drop your arms. Now hold 'em up or do I need to give you another demonstration?"

"No, mister. Please don't hurt me again. I won't cause you any trouble."

Crudder moved over to Hopper and rapidly pulled his dagger

from the wounded shoulder. Hopper doubled over in pain. He wiped the dagger on Hopper's shirt and returned it to its home.

"Sit down and hold your shirt over the wound. Otherwise you'll bleed out in just a few minutes."

As Hopper sat on the edge of his bed, John picked up Hopper's fancy dress shirt and tied it to the injured shoulder to staunch the flow of blood.

"I heard enough to know you were the mastermind behind the kidnapping. Tell me why? Why Charley Ross? Why take a child in Philadelphia? That seems like a lot of trouble. You could have done the same thing here with less risk."

Hopper snarled. "But Ross is not in New York. I was willing to do whatever it took to hurt him."

"What have you got against Mr. Ross?" asked Crudder.

"He was my partner. We built the business together and then he forced me out. He said I had cheated our customers. I lost everything in just a few days. When I lost my business, my wife divorced me and took the kids with her. Do you know what it's like to lose your children? They were my life. I loved nothing more than coming home at night and having my children run to me and jump into my arms. How wonderful to hear them yell, 'Daddy's home' I'll never get to hear that again."

"So, this is about revenge?" asked Crudder.

"Revenge—and money. I hope Christian Ross is broken-hearted as he wonders what happened to little Charley."

John listened hoping Hopper would reveal more about what was behind the kidnapping and where Charley was. "What was

Boseman's role?"

"All he had to do was keep an eye on the investigation and mail some letters. I didn't think he could mess that up but he did. And if he hadn't come here, you never would've known about me."

"That may well be right. I'm just glad Boseman led me here." John pulled a chair up in front of Hopper and looked him in the eyes. "Tell me where Charley Ross is."

The corner of Hopper's lip turned up as he considered Crudder's question. "I don't know. Mosher is the only one who knows. And if he hired others to help as I told him to, he may not even know where the boy is."

"What's Mosher's first name?"

"Stop with the questions," said Hopper. "My shoulder is throbbing. I need to go to the hospital."

"Just a few more questions and I'll get you the care you need. Now what is Mosher's first name?"

"I don't know. Seems like it's…I can't remember…Bill. That's it. Bill Mosher."

"What does he look like?"

"He's got the bushiest sideburns I've ever seen. They're mostly white. But he has something wrong with his nose. It's just sort of a lump. No shape to it."

"How did you pick Mosher for the job. Did you know him before the kidnapping?"

"I'd never heard of him. I was down at the waterfront and overheard someone saying he had just been let out of jail. I heard he was broke and the word on him was he would do anything for money. He lived on a boat so it was easy for me to watch him from the shore. As I watched his interactions with people, I realized he was smart and ambitious. I watched him use card tricks to cheat people out of their money. One night I followed him as he went to a house on shore and broke in. He was fearless! I couldn't believe he would just break into a house like that." Hopper grimaced before he continued.

"That's when I knew I had the right man. So, the next day, I wrote a note promising him a lot of money for a job and if he wanted to hear about it, he'd meet me at a bar down the road. Sure enough, he was there, eager for anything I suggested."

"What happened next?"

"I laid 10 one hundred-dollar bills on the table and told him it was for expenses. You would've thought his eyes were going to pop right out of his head. He salivated looking at the money. I realized I could have asked him to kill someone for me and he probably would've done it. He was hungry and greedy. What a loser."

John thought it interesting that Hopper referred to his associates as idiots and losers. It sure seemed to Crudder, Hopper was in the same group as the rest of the kidnappers. "How many people are involved in this?"

"The only people I hired were Mosher and Boseman. It doesn't sound like Boseman hired anyone else but I know Mosher did. When we met and I explained what I wanted him to do, he said he wanted to hire two or three men to help. I don't have any idea who he hired. Boseman was to keep watch on him and let me know when the ransom was paid."

Hopper complained about his wounded shoulder as he bent forward holding his injured wing. "This hurts like the devil. You've ruined my shoulder."

"Sit back down, Hopper."

"I just need to move. It hurts so bad." John watched as he moved across the room bent low and complaining loudly.

"I said sit down."

Hopper ignored the direction and continued to complain about the pain. Crudder watched him move over to a table.

"Hopper, this is not going to end well if you don't sit down."

When Hopper got to the table, he reached below a folded cloth and came up with a gun.

"Don't do it, Hopper."

As Hopper spun toward Crudder with the gun in his hand, John used his left hand to withdraw and throw the other dagger he kept on his back. In one fluid motion, John ended Hopper's life. He stood over the body and shook his head. John stepped forward and removed the dagger from the dead man's chest and wiped the blade on Hopper's shirt.

Replacing the dagger in its sheath, Crudder removed his hat and said a silent prayer. *Lord, I know the President would be glad I saved our country the pain of this man standing trial, but you know my heart. I wanted to bring him back to the authorities. I commend him to your care. There must be a special punishment waiting for those who would take a child. A-men.*

John walked out the back door and nonchalantly walked down

the alley to his buggy. He thought: *Two down and three or four more to go.*

CHAPTER 27

Tuesday, July 28th

Crudder took a late train back to Philadelphia and made it to the police station early Tuesday morning. The day shift was just coming on duty. He made his way back to Dixon's office.

"There you are," said Sergeant Dixon. "Where have you been since Saturday? I thought you would have been around here more."

"There's time for that in a minute, Sergeant. Did the Pinkertons get here?"

"Yes, they did. This is the first time I've worked with them. I think they're every bit as good as their reputation."

"Was Allen Pinkerton with them?"

"Yes, he came and brought nine other men. He said he would provide any additional men we needed. They're in the process of interviewing everyone in Christian Ross's neighborhood.

"He asked if I would agree for him to bring in twenty more men. John, I told him to bring them in. Honestly, they have much more experience with investigations than my men, except for Detective Ramsey. They should be here this morning. Mr. Pinkerton said he thought they would be best utilized continuing to interview everyone who might have seen anything or have knowledge of Charley's whereabouts."

"That sounds like a good plan," said Crudder. "What have you found out so far?"

"I didn't think we were making much progress, but the Pinkerton men found several people who saw the buggy and gave a pretty good description of the two men. I've had our artist drawing pictures of the two men based on those descriptions. I was just getting ready to take them to the printer." Dixon handed the drawings to Crudder. Both men were young. Dixon told him one of the men had red hair.

"Sergeant, I think these are local men who were hired to take part in the kidnapping, but I also think there are other men involved. Do these descriptions fit what you found from all of the witnesses?"

"All except for Mr. Ross's neighbor, Miss Mary Kidder. She insisted on completely different descriptions. She said one of the men was skinny—rail-thin, she called him. And the other man had thick sideburns and a funny nose. But she can't be right. The rest of the descriptions favor the drawings I have here."

"Did you ever consider there could be another team of men involved?"

Dixon shook his head. "No, I just thought Miss Kidder was mixed up. She is getting older."

"She may be older, Sergeant. But she gave a good description of a boatbuilder from New York City named Bill Mosher. He's the man Hopper hired to carry out the kidnapping. He was instructed to hire as many men as he needed to carry out the crime. He told Hopper he thought he needed two or three additional men."

Dixon stroked his chin as he considered what Crudder had told him.

"Who's Hopper?"

"Sorry, Sergeant. Harrison Hopper is the man who hired Boseman. I traced Boseman to Hopper's home in New York City. According to Hopper, Mosher is the man he hired to take Charley. I want to get an artist and get a drawing based on the description I was given. It'll be interesting to see if Walter Ross recognizes him as the Candy Man."

"There is an artist right down the street that we have used before. She does a great job." Dixon got up from his desk and led Crudder outside of the police station and down the street to the artist. After introductions were made, the young woman listened to John's description and rapidly drew, making minor adjustments as John directed.

"That's Bill Mosher, at least as far as the description I've received. But the nose is wrong. Draw the nose as though it were missing the cartilage that gives it shape. It's been described to me as being more of a lump." The artist made the change and presented it to Crudder.

"I think that'll do for now. Sergeant, we need to dispatch someone to take this to the Pinkerton office in New York. Then get them to hire another artist to make whatever changes are necessary based on descriptions from those who know Mosher. Also, get them to find out about any known associates of Mosher's."

Crudder followed Dixon back to his office. "Sergeant, has anyone outside the station seen the drawings of the men in the buggy?"

"Not yet. I was going to get them printed and start distributing them around the city."

"That's good, Sergeant. But I think you need to start closer to home. If the drawings are of local men, I think it's likely one of your officers has had contact with them. I know you'll want to show them when they come back with reports at the end of the day."

Dixon pulled the pad from his pocket and made a note. "I can't believe I didn't think of that."

"Also, as soon as you get the first posters printed, get someone over to the jail to see if any of your jailers recognize them. My guess is, we'll know the identity of these men before the end of the day."

The Sergeant made another notation on his pocket pad and stared at Crudder in amazement. "It sounds like you've made a lot of progress yourself. How'd you find out about Mosher?"

"Things you told me about Boseman just didn't make sense to me. It sounded like he was more interested in keeping up with your progress than he was with helping with the investigation. I also found out from Christian Ross that he was charging only one dollar a day for his services, well below the standard for that kind of work."

"I certainly didn't know that. It would've made me suspicious."

Crudder continued. "I pressed him on his involvement in the kidnapping. He denied it, of course. But after convincing him I was going to see him arrested for the kidnapping, he fled to New York City. I trailed him there and overheard him meeting with Hopper. As it turns out, Hopper was Ross's partner in business but got pushed out by Ross for cheating customers. As a result, his wife left him and took his children. He said he wanted Ross to know what it was like to lose a child."

"Did you get the New York Police to arrest Hopper?"

"No, Sergeant. Something else you need to know. Boseman is the one who has been sending the letters. I'm not sure if he sent them all but I do know that was his primary job."

"Where is Boseman now?"

"Hopper murdered him. I didn't get there in time to stop him."

"What else did you find out from Hopper?"

"He said he hired Mosher and promised him half of the twenty thousand they demanded from Ross. My guess is, he never had intention of paying him. He promised Boseman three thousand dollars so he could get away. But when Boseman went to collect it, Hopper killed him."

Dixon shook his head. "How did you accomplish so much in such a short time?"

Crudder ignored the question. "Mosher is a boat builder who lives on his boat in New York. I'm going to get the Pinkertons to see what they can find out about him."

"What about Hopper?"

"We don't need to worry about him," said Crudder. "He's no longer a factor."

"Is he in jail?"

"No. He's been neutralized."

"What does that mean?"

"It means he's been eliminated."

"But I don't understand," said Dixon.

"Sergeant, you'll not need to worry about him anymore. Got it?"

Slowly Dixon nodded his head as he realized what John was saying.

"Get Allen Pinkerton to dig up everything they can about Mosher. They may find something that will be helpful. I think the focus of our work needs to be finding the two men who took Charley. What have you done in that regard?"

Dixon stuttered a bit as he tried to give a report he knew was going to be inadequate. "We...we...well, I've just gotten the descriptions of the two men. I was going to...I mean I planned on sending men out to look for them."

"That sounds fine, Sergeant. Assuming these are the two men who have Charley, where will you concentrate your search?"

"Each person who gave us descriptions said the buggy was traveling north. Do you think that's where we need to focus?"

"Perhaps. Sergeant, you said several letters have been received. We know now that Boseman sent them. Can you show me on a map where they were mailed from?"

Dixon walked up to a wall map of Philadelphia. "Well, there were three letters from outside of Philadelphia. One from New York, one from New Brunswick, and one from the Hudson Valley." Then the sergeant pointed to various places on the Philadelphia map. "They were mailed from here, here, and here, but I can't recall all of the locations off hand."

Dixon consulted the pad in his pocket that contained his notes of the case. He then took pins with short but bright orange ribbons attached and began sticking them in the map at various places. When he was through, he stepped back and was amazed to find the letters were from nearly all parts of the city. But there were no flags in the northern part of the city and none outside the city to the north.

"John, I never would've thought to mark the mailboxes where the letters were mailed. It seems clear, they've been trying to steer us away from looking to the north."

"I think you're right, Sergeant. And judging from what you've told me about your search so far, it may be time to start moving beyond the city limits."

"I'll start dividing up the area north of the city into sectors," said Dixon. "As each team checks in, I'll reassign them to that region. Allen Pinkerton is down the hall. I'll tell him so he can concentrate his men there as well."

Sergeant Dixon paused and thought about how the investigation had changed in the few minutes John had been in his office. "John, thank you for your work. Earlier this morning, I didn't feel a real sense of direction. But with your help, I think we now are on the right track."

"You're welcome, Sergeant. I certainly hope we're reading the signs correctly."

✳ ✳ ✳

Later that afternoon, one of the policemen returned from the central jail with a report for Sergeant Dixon.

"I showed the poster around the jail and it seems everyone knew them. Both men were just released a few weeks ago. The red headed young man is named Rusty Rhodes. He's a small-time hoodlum. The other is named Harry "Slick" Stegall. It seems Stegall enlisted Rhodes to help him burglarize houses throughout the city. They have both been released on bail pending their trial."

"Where are they now?" asked Dixon.

"No one knows. Stegall was released one day and Rhodes the next. Neither has been seen since then. The word is they are always looking for a way to get money without having to work for it."

CHAPTER 28

Friday, August 14th

Cave, North of Philadelphia

lick Stegall was tired of babysitting. Little Charley cried most of the time. Some of the time he screamed as though something was hurting him. When he wasn't screaming, he was calling for his mother.

Rusty Rhodes felt he had more patience than Slick but he was also sick of listening to the little boy scream throughout much of the night. Rusty tried to get him to eat breakfast. All Charley would do was push the plate away and say, "No."

"Come on, Charley. You've got to eat something." Rusty's voice took on an edge as he lost his patience with the little boy.

"No," shouted Charley as he pushed his plate away.

"I've had just about enough of that. You're going to eat. You hear me?" yelled Rusty. He grabbed little Charley and shook him hard. Charley cried all the louder. *He's as spoiled as my little brother!*

Stegall watched in horror as Rusty Rhodes threw Charley to the ground. The little boy's head hit the ground with great force and his body went limp. "What have you done?" yelled Slick.

Rusty turned the other way and put his hands to his head.

"You've killed him! Now Bill is going to kill us. Have you lost your mind?"

Rusty pulled a gun from his waistband, turned back and shot Stegall in the chest. Slick looked down at his shirt with the growing bloom of red. Shock registered on his face as he died and fell forward. He looked over at the child and accepted Slick's assessment that the little boy was dead.

Rusty wasn't sure what to do next. He realized Mosher would likely be in a murderous rage if he reported Slick and the little boy were both dead. Rusty bent over Slick's body and went through his pockets. He was happy to find he had most of the advance Mosher had paid plus another fifty dollars. That wasn't as much as he was counting on but he knew it was all he was going to get for his trouble.

He hitched the buggy and headed back toward Philadelphia. He passed through a little town named Plymouth Meeting that had a livery stable, a saloon, and a hotel. Rusty traded the buggy rig for a saddle horse and tack, went to the saloon and got a bottle of whisky. He then got a room for the night and plotted his next steps.

CHAPTER 29

Tuesday, August 18th
Philadelphia, Pennsylvania

For the previous two weeks, Crudder independently followed up leads that were not being pursued by the police department or the Pinkerton detectives. He started out looking north of the city. After several days with nothing to show for his efforts, he started focusing on the east. Several days of fruitless search caused him to turn his attention to the west and the south.

Good police work had resulted in finding the hotel where Mosher and his gang of kidnappers planned their crime. Their rooms were still rented but not being used. After more than two weeks of surveillance, the detectives presumed the gang had moved on. Crudder agreed with their assessment.

On the morning of August eighteenth, Crudder thought again about how early in the investigation the kidnappers were trying to influence the investigators to think they went anywhere except north. Even though the Pinkertons had long since abandoned the possibility the boy could have been taken north, John decided he would return to that area and concentrate his focus there unless something more promising presented itself.

Armed with posters of Stegall and Rhodes, Crudder stopped in every town, every business, and every home he encountered. Several of the people he talked with said they had seen the two men but there were no recent sightings.

When he got to Plymouth Meeting, a small town founded more than a hundred years before, he showed the posters to the stableman at the livery.

"Well, one of them is in town now. There's a redheaded young man who traded me a buggy and horse for that buckskin over there. He's been here for several days. I don't know why he's still around."

"Any idea where I could find him?" asked Crudder.

"I've seen him coming out of the saloon several times. And I'm guessing he's staying in the hotel."

Crudder thanked him and walked over to the saloon. He looked over the swinging doors and spotted a redheaded man at the end of the bar. He had a half-full bottle of whisky in front of him. John pulled his gun and started walking slowly toward Rusty.

The bartender saw John and hollered. "Watch out, Rusty."

The young man pulled his gun from his waistband and fired as he was turning toward Crudder. John shot in self-defense and watched Rhodes sink to the floor. The bartender ducked behind the bar for a gun when Crudder yelled after him. "Don't do it.

Federal agent. I'm here to arrest this man. You've butted in where you weren't welcome."

The bartender quickly stood and raised his hands. "I'm sorry, mister. I didn't know you were the law. I thought you were just picking on young Rusty."

John went to Rusty's bleeding body and kicked his gun out of the way. The young man looked to be about twenty-seven or twenty-eight, the same as John.

"Rusty, where is the boy. Where're you keeping Charley Ross?" John thought how in other circumstances, they might even have been friends. How could lives turn out so differently? Was it where they were raised or who raised them? Did Rusty's background somehow inure him to a life of crime? Would John have turned out the same way given the same circumstances?

Rusty coughed as blood came out of his mouth. "He's—dead. Didn't mean to. He—wouldn't—stop crying. Tried to—make—him—stop. I—didn't—mean—to—kill— him."

"Where's Stegall?" asked Crudder.

Rusty struggled to talk. "Dead. Got—tired—of him—bossing—me." With those words, Rusty breathed his last.

Roy Clinton

CHAPTER 30

Wednesday, August 19th
Philadelphia, Pennsylvania

John was stunned by what had taken place. Despite all that had been done to bring little Charley Ross home safely, the kidnapping had come to the worst possible conclusion. Crudder made arrangements to bury the young man and headed back to Philadelphia early the following morning.

When he got to the police station, he realized the day shift had not yet been given their assignments. He went to tell Sergeant Dixon what he had learned.

"Morning, John," said Dixon. "Something has happened since I saw you last."

"What's that, Sergeant?"

"P.T. Barnum came to town and offered Christian Ross ten thousand dollars if he would allow Charley to join his circus after he is found."

"That's ludicrous. Surely, Ross didn't accept the offer."

"Actually, he did," said Dixon. "It turns out Ross needed the money. He took Barnum's money and agreed to tour the country with Charley as a sideshow exhibit."

Crudder shook his head. He couldn't believe Ross would be so desperate for money that he would agree to such a preposterous offer.

"Why the long face?" asked Dixon.

"I'm afraid I have some bad news." He went into the sergeant's office and closed the door, placed his hat on the desk, and dropped into a chair. "I've just come from Plymouth Meeting. Charley Ross is dead."

"What? How'd it happen?"

"I got a line on Rusty Rhodes in that town. He was in a saloon when I went to arrest him. The bartender interfered and Rusty pulled his gun. I had no choice but to shoot him."

"What about the boy?"

"Before he died, Rhodes admitted to killing the boy because he got tired of his crying. It sounds like he lost his temper and in a moment of rage killed him."

"Did you find Stegall?"

"Rhodes said he was tired of being bossed around by Stegall so he killed him as well."

The sergeant slumped behind his desk. Crudder put his head into his hands, sad to know Charley Ross would not be returned to his family.

"So where does that leave us?" asked Dixon.

"We still need to find Mosher. Have you turned up anything on him?"

"We know he's not in the hotel where he's registered," said Dixon. "Several of the staff remember seeing him but no one has seen him for the past several weeks. My guess is he's moved on to a different part of the country. I don't know if we'll ever catch him."

"We have to. With Charley Ross dead, we must tie up this last loose end. We do know Mosher is the one who kidnapped the boy. I think the only way the family will ever find peace is to know the kidnapper has been brought to justice."

"I've got to get to roll call. Will you tell the men what you told me? I think they need to hear first-hand what took place." John agreed and followed Dixon to the assembly room.

"All right men, settle down for roll call." The sergeant quickly called the names of the men and noted the few absences. "Before I get to the assignments for the day, I want to call on Agent Crudder. He's just given me some news I've asked him to pass on to you."

Crudder stood before the policemen. He guessed there were close to two hundred men in the room. "I'm afraid I have some bad news," he began. "Charley Ross is dead."

There was a collective groan throughout the room as the men realized their hard work in trying to find the little boy had all come to naught.

"I tracked down Rusty Rhodes yesterday in Plymouth Meeting. When I went into a saloon to arrest him, the bartender warned him and Rhodes pulled his gun and shot at me. I had no choice but to shoot him. Before he died, he admitted to killing the boy in a fit of rage. He said he had also killed Stegall."

The noise in the assembly room picked up as the policemen talked to each other. "Quiet down," said Sergeant Dixon. "Tell them the rest, John."

"Several of you had met a private detective named Boseman who'd been hired by Christian Ross. As it turns out, Boseman was part of the kidnapping. He was the one who mailed the ransom letters. I let Boseman escape in hopes of trailing him. I was able to follow him to New York City to the man who planned the kidnapping. His name is Harrison Hopper. He was a business partner of Christian Ross but got forced out for cheating customers. He hired a boatbuilder named Bill Mosher to commit the kidnapping. Mosher was promised half of the twenty-thousand-dollar ransom but Hopper never had intentions of paying him.

"Hopper murdered Boseman to keep from paying him off. I confronted Hopper and was arresting him but was forced to kill him. The remaining loose end is Bill Mosher and anyone else he may have hired to help with the kidnapping."

"Thank you, John," said Sergeant Dixon. He then continued the report to his men. "We know Mosher hasn't been seen in Philadelphia for at least three weeks. That doesn't mean he's not here. As you go out on your assignments today, make sure you take posters of Mosher. If he's in the city, I want to get him. That's all. Now get moving and find Mosher."

CHAPTER 31

Sunday, August 23rd
New York City

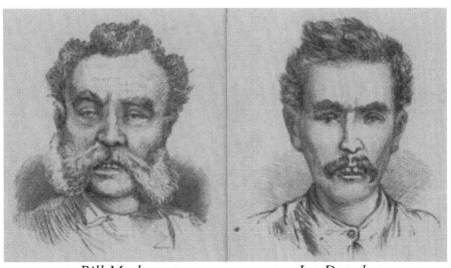

Bill Mosher   *Joe Douglas*

Photos from the New York Public Library

The Pinkerton detectives had completed their interviews of everyone who had ever heard of Mosher. They had been able to fine-tune the description of Mosher and got a new drawing made. The detectives were also able to learn he had been seen in the company of a petty thief named Joe Douglas. With the help of the New York City police department, they were able to get a detailed description of Douglas. Posters of both men were distributed throughout the city.

In late August, Mosher and Douglas were spotted boarding Mosher's boat, which had remained under surveillance. Word was sent to John Crudder to see how he wanted them to proceed.

John Crudder
c/o Police Department
Philadelphia, Pennsylvania

Mosher and Douglas have moved into Mosher's boat. Awaiting further instructions.

Allan Pinkerton
Pinkerton Agency
New York City

Sergeant Dixon received the telegram late in the day and took it to Crudder's hotel. John wrote out a response for the sergeant to send on his behalf.

Alan Pinkerton
Pinkerton Agency
New York City

*Surveil only. Do not apprehend unless they try to escape.
Expect my arrival in NYC at midday tomorrow.*

*John Crudder
c/o Police Department
Philadelphia, Pennsylvania*

John knew the last train for New York had departed. He decided to get as much sleep as he could and head to New York the next morning. When he arrived, he went immediately to the police station and was brought up to date.

"Mr. Crudder," said Captain Emerson. "We appreciate you coming. I'm afraid there have been some developments since we last communicated with you."

Crudder followed the captain back to his office and took an offered seat. "As it turns out, one of our own has been involved in the kidnapping. We've just arrested William Westervelt. I'm pained to admit, he used to be a New York City cop. He's the brother-in-law of Bill Mosher. He's been keeping Mosher informed. Because of that, Mosher has successfully evaded our attempts at capturing him. Thanks to the Pinkertons, we've had eyes on him for the past several days."

"Douglas is still with him?" asked Crudder.

"That's right. We think they're getting ready for a robbery or burglary."

"Why do you say that?"

"Each time they've come off the boat, they've driven past

various homes and businesses. They appear to be trying to make up their minds as to their target."

"Is there anything in the record of either man that gives you an indication of the type of target they are looking for?"

Captain Emerson nodded. "Most of their previous arrests have been for burglarizing homes. They target affluent neighborhoods and select houses where it appears no one is home."

"How many nights have they been staking out houses?" asked Crudder.

"They checked out some businesses for one night but for the past two nights, they have concentrated on houses."

"Did they go to the same neighborhood each time?"

"Yes, they did. In fact, they have been focusing on Justice Charles Van Brunt's house. We think there is a good chance they'll try a break in there before long."

"Is the judge living there now?"

"Yes, he is. That's given us some concern. We went to see the judge this morning and suggested he and his family move out for a few days. We really think Mosher and Douglas might make a play for the house tonight."

"Captain Emerson, thanks for waiting until I got to town to make a move on those two. What I'm wondering is if we're taking unnecessary chances waiting for him to commit a burglary. We have plenty of evidence to arrest him for kidnapping. And now since Charley Ross is dead, there will be murder charges."

"That's true," said the captain. "But if we're not successful in tying them to the murder of the boy, we think we stand a better chance of getting them back in custody if we can catch them in the act of a burglary."

"I guess that makes sense," said Crudder. "Kidnapping is only a misdemeanor whereas burglary is a felony. Until I got on this case, I didn't realize kidnapping is a misdemeanor in every state. But I was also surprised to find there's no federal statute against kidnapping."

"We've assigned two teams to stake out the judge's house tonight. I assume you want to be included."

'Yes, I do, Captain. Thanks."

"I'm planning on leading one team," said the captain. "Would you like to lead the other one?

"Yes, I would. Just tell me how you want to do this."

"We have asked the families on each side of the judge's house to stay inside and out of sight tonight. As it turns out, one house will be vacant. We can put a team in there and have the other team watching the back of the house. The judge's brother, Holmes Van Brunt, lives on one side and he'll be home tonight. However, they should not be a concern.

"I figured we need to be in place by five. I also have a team of three men watching Mosher's boat. Assuming they make their move tonight, that team will trail them to the judge's house."

"Captain, it's crucial that we capture Mosher and Douglas alive. So far, everyone who has been associated with the kidnapping is dead. We must be able to question them to understand what was behind the crime. President Grant has been very clear that all possible means be taken to ensure such a crime doesn't happen again."

"What are you suggesting, Mr. Crudder?" John detected the defensiveness in the captain's voice. And suddenly addressing him as Mr. Crudder instead of John confirmed that wariness.

"I don't intend to tell you how to do police work. But I do believe you need to make it clear to your men that Mosher and Douglas must be taken alive."

"Thank you, Mr. Crudder. I will pass that word along."

CHAPTER 32

Shortly before midnight, Mosher and Douglas made their move. They left the boat and took the buggy to Justice Van Brunt's house. Nothing had changed since their previous surveillance. The house looked deserted, which suited Mosher. He was skilled at burglary but didn't like breaking into an occupied home. Douglas, for his part, was a follower. It didn't matter to him if people were home or not. All he cared about was getting his share of the loot.

Douglas stopped the buggy down the block from the Van Brunt home. The two criminals walked down to the targeted home, noting nothing of interest. As far as Mosher could tell, the other houses on the block were either unoccupied or everyone was asleep.

They went to the back door of Van Brunt's home and Douglas jimmied the lock. Immediately, an alarm bell began to ring.

"What do we do now?" Douglas turned to run but Mosher

caught him.

"We keep going. We can clean the place out before the police get here. Don't panic."

Reluctantly, Douglas turned back into the house. They lit the lantern they were carrying and began searching the house. The two men wasted no time going to the second floor and removing valuables from the bedrooms. Then they came downstairs to finish their job.

The teams of police held their place with the intent of arresting Mosher and Douglas when they exited the home. However, the judge's brother decided to take matters into his own hands.

Holmes Van Brant and his son, Albert, enlisted the aid of two gardeners. All four men were armed with shotguns. They slipped over to the judge's house to wait. When they saw a lantern in the window, Holmes gave a signal to open the door. All four men attacked and discharged their shotguns into Mosher and Douglas.

Mosher died immediately and Douglas was mortally wounded. Crudder ran to the house as he heard the gunfire. He pulled his six gun and cautiously approached. He realized Mosher was gone but Douglas was still moving.

Crudder bent down and lifted Douglas's head into his lap. "Joe, can you hear me?"

Douglas's eyes opened and he gasped for a breath. "I—hear—you."

"Where is the boy? Where is Charley Ross?"

"Gone—We—got—."

Crudder shook Douglas. "Don't drift away on me, Douglas. Did you and Mosher take Charley?"

"We—took—him. Gone."

"What do you mean, gone?"

"He's—gone. Dead."

With those words, Joe Douglas breathed his last. Crudder shook him again. "Joe! Don't die on me. Where's Charley?"

John placed Joe's head back on the floor. The captain approached and looked down at Douglas. "Good riddance is all I can say."

Crudder stood and angrily confronted the policeman. "Do you realize what you're saying? Douglas is the last one who could tell us anything about the kidnapping."

"The boy's dead," said Captain Emerson. "Douglas couldn't tell us anything more."

"One thing's for certain. He can't tell us anything more now. We needed them both alive. There's so much we don't know about this crime. I wanted to question him. At the very least, we could have found out where they kept the boy."

"You're right, Crudder. I do wish he was still alive. It's bad enough for Mr. Ross to have his son killed. But it's much worse for him to not even be able to bury him."

Crudder stood and removed his hat as he looked down at Douglas. Silently he prayed. *Lord, I don't know how someone could get as misguided as Douglas. He's in your care now. Do with him as you see best. A-men.*

"Captain, I won't be at the station tomorrow. My work here is done. Please communicate with Allen Pinkerton and let him know their work is over. I'll be making my report to President Grant."

"Mr. Crudder," said the captain in a voice that was close to panic, "I hope you won't mention my comment to the President. I just wasn't thinking. I meant no harm."

"Goodbye, Captain." Crudder left the Van Brunt home and went to his hotel. Back in his room, he felt as though he had completely failed in his mission. Not only was Charley Ross dead but he was not even successful in recovering the body.

He lay in his bed that night trying to sleep but sleep wouldn't come. When morning came, he would write a letter to the President telling him the outcome and then travel back to Bandera, Texas. He wasn't sure what else he could have done to have changed the outcome but still he was not able to shake his sense of failure.

CHAPTER 33

Monday, August 24th
Philadelphia, Pennsylvania

John went to Grand Central Depot with the intention of heading directly back home. He went to the telegraph office and sent a message to Charlotte.

Charlotte Crudder
Bandera, Texas

Headed home. Will be there in three weeks or less. Love to you and the girls.

John Crudder
New York City, New York

Prior to purchasing his ticket, he went to a secluded part of the depot and wrote the President but addressed the envelope to the

President's assistant, Jeffrey Jameson.

Dear Mr. President,

I'm sad to report that Charley Ross is dead. One of the kidnappers, Rusty Rhodes, admitted to killing the boy and killing his partner, Harry "Slick" Stegall.

Bill Mosher was hired by the disgruntled former partner of Christian Ross, Harrison Hopper, to kidnap the boy. Mosher hired Joe Douglas as his initial partner. He then hired Rhodes and Stegall to hide the boy. Private detective, Arthur Boseman, was also hired by Hopper to keep track of the progress of the police and to write the ransom letters.

Hopper killed Boseman to keep from paying him. Mosher and Douglas died last night in a botched burglary. Prior to his death, Douglas admitted he and Mosher took the boy and confirmed that Charley had been killed. I killed Rhodes and Hopper.

Having failed at my mission of rescuing Charley Ross, I feel have no choice but to tender my resignation as your Special Agent.

It has been my privilege to serve you in this capacity. I wish you every continued success in your presidency.

I have a strong belief kidnapping should be a federal offense. While not being sure how to proceed with this, I wanted to impress upon you the importance of such a law.

Sincerely,
John Crudder

John put down his pen, folded the letter and addressed the envelope. He purchased postage at the post office inside the depot and dropped it in the mailbox. Crudder took a seat and silently calculated how long it would take him to get back to Bandera. As much as he wanted to get home, he felt his business was still unfinished.

He went to the ticket window to book the first leg of his trip home. "I'd like a ticket for Kansas City." The clerk was busy getting his ticket when he changed his mind. "Second thought, make that a ticket to Philadelphia." The train was leaving within the hour.

When he got on board, he was uncertain of all that would happen when he got there but he knew he needed to meet with Mr. Ross. Lost in thought, Crudder wondered how he would ever be able to apologize for not bringing Charley Ross home. He pictured his twin daughters and how grateful he was they were in his life.

Before Crudder expected it, the train pulled into the station in Philadelphia. He only had one small bag, having given away most of the additional clothes he had purchased while on the case. John found there was a train leaving for Kansas City late in the afternoon so he purchased a ticket and arranged to leave his bag with the ticket agent until he returned. He felt his business in Philadelphia wouldn't take him long.

CHAPTER 34

Crudder hired a horse and checked his notes for the Ross address. John recalled the directions to Germantown and set out for what he thought would be the most difficult meeting of his life.

He found his way back to East Washington Lane and reluctantly directed his horse down the street. Crudder once again realized how the front wall and the many thick trees in the yard worked in the kidnapper's favor. John tied his horse to the hitching rail and took the brick walk to the front door. As he drew back his fist to knock, the door opened.

"Come in, Mr. Crudder," said Christian Ross.

John removed his hat. "You startled me, Mr. Ross. I hope I didn't disturb you."

"You didn't disturb me at all. When I'm home, I've taken to sitting in the front room so I can see what's happening in the neighborhood. If only I had that habit months ago, perhaps

Charley would still be with me."

Crudder didn't know what to say so he stood on the porch with his hat in his hand. "Please excuse my poor manners. Please come in Mr. Crudder."

"Just call me John, Mr. Ross."

"And you call me Christian." John followed Mr. Ross into the parlor and took the seat that was offered.

"How can I help you, John? If you've come to tell me about Charley, you can save your words. Sergeant Dixon's already told me he's dead." Ross put his hands to his face and cried out loud. Tears dripped between his fingers. When he composed himself, John attempted to find the words he had rehearsed on his trip from New York.

"Mr. Ross, I was hoping to have a few minutes to speak to you and your wife."

"I'm afraid my wife is still out of town. And after Charley's death, I'm not sure she wants to come back home."

John nodded his head as an acknowledgment of what Ross had said. Crudder began and then paused and cleared his throat. "I'm not sure I know how to say what's on my mind. I've been rehearsing a speech for you on my train trip here from New York. But I can't recall any of it now."

John Crudder looked at his boots and rolled his hat in his hands. "The bottom line is I failed you. I was sent here as an agent of the President of the United States. My job was to solve the kidnapping and bring your son home. Part of me wants to say I know how you feel. But I don't. I'm a father but if something happened to one of my children I'm sure I would feel like the world just ended for me."

Crudder shuffled his feet and continued. "Mr. Ross, Christian, I owe you a deeper apology than I'm able to give. And please don't misunderstand me. I'm not looking for forgiveness. I don't deserve that. But you shouldn't have to suffer because of my failure."

John looked back at his boots and continued rolling his hat. "Just so you know, I have already written the President and resigned as his *Special Agent*. No one else should ever have to suffer as you have because of my failure." John stood and waited a few awkward seconds as he mutilated his hat. "Well, I guess that's about it. Thank you for seeing me, Mr. Ross."

Crudder turned and walked out of the house and off the grand porch. When he got to the steps, Ross called after him. "John, I did you the favor of listening to what you had to say. I'm going to ask the same courtesy from you. I have a few things to say."

"I apologize again, Christian. You're absolutely right. I do indeed want to listen to what you have to say."

"Then come back in and have a seat. I didn't prepare a speech as you did but I have plenty to say." Crudder obediently followed Ross back to the parlor and took a seat.

"John, you said you didn't know how I felt. I'm going to try to tell you. I feel like I have been punched in the gut again and again. The pain is so great, I have trouble breathing. When I try to sleep, all I can think about is Charley and wonder how he was treated before he was murdered. When I close my eyes, I get a vision of a bully taking my boy and then violently ending his life. I try to eat but I don't have any appetite." Christian's eyes brimmed with tears as he talked about his feelings.

"A couple of times I've forced myself to eat, knowing I'll not survive if I don't. But after a few bites, I throw up. Walter is still staying with a neighbor. I know it would not be good for him to be around me right now. Our nanny takes care of the baby. John, I know this sounds bad but right now I don't care about Walter or the baby.

"I received a letter from my wife and she flatly said she doesn't see any reason to come home. She's thinking about moving to Atlantic City and asked me when I could get Walter and the baby ready to move there. Everything that's been important to me is evaporating.

"You know something of my financial situation. But what most people don't know is I am worse than dead broke. Every month, I incur more debt trying to keep this house and the lifestyle my family has grown used to. But with my wife not coming home, I don't need this house any more. Truthfully, I don't think I'll ever be able to come into this house without thinking of Charley and how his death is partially my fault. If I wasn't so obsessed with having more trees than anyone else and having the wall in front of the house, Charley would never have ended up in that wagon.

"In the next few days, I'm going to put the house up for sale and go see my wife. I'm going to try to salvage my marriage. But I know she blames me for Charley's death. She may never be able to get beyond that."

Christian paused for several moments and then looked directly at John. "Before Charley died, the thing that nagged at me more than anything else was not knowing why Charley was taken. I couldn't understand why anyone would pick him. John, thanks to you, I don't have to wonder any longer. It's because of you I found out Harrison Hopper planned the whole thing. He was angry that I found out he was cheating customers. Without you, I would've forever wondered why anyone would take Charley.

"Knowing why he was taken and who was behind it doesn't make me grieve Charley's loss any less, but it does answer those questions. And John, it's because of you, all who took place in the kidnapping have been eliminated."

Anger burned in Ross's eyes. He wiped the tears and looked steadfastly at Crudder. "John, thank you for ending Hopper's life. I just wish I had been there to see it. Your actions give me a sense of satisfaction. Men who would commit such crimes should not be allowed to live."

Crudder nodded his head in agreement but said nothing. "Well, that's about all I have to say. John, I don't believe you failed at all. Because of you, those bad men no longer draw breath. I will always wish Charley was still alive but I will forever be grateful you handed out justice to those who deserved no mercy."

John nodded in gratitude. After several seconds of silence, the men stood. Christian extended his hand and John took it. John turned and left the house. As he rode back to the train station, he had a number or conflicting feelings. He was still consumed with a sense of failure. But listening to the words of Christian, he realized he had indeed accomplished much of what he had started out to do. Still, nothing would take away his despair in knowing Charley Ross didn't get a chance to grow up and fully live his life.

* * *

John stopped by the telegraph office in the train station to send a message to his money manager back in New York. He was moved by the financial reversal suffered by the Ross family and wanted to do something for them. Pausing to compose his thoughts, he then took pen in hand and wrote out his message. He signed it cryptically in the off chance the telegraph operator was tempted to reveal his identity to Ross.

Howard Hastings
Fifth Avenue
New York City, New York

Send $50,000 to Christian Ross, Philadelphia, Pennsylvania, with note, "From one father to another," and sign it, Anonymous.

M^2
Philadelphia, Pennsylvania

Rather than feeling good about his philanthropic act, he was conflicted. He wondered how much of his action was based on his own guilt or on his desire to make himself feel better. Deep inside, he knew his only desire was to help someone who had suffered greatly.

Roy Clinton

CHAPTER 35

Friday, August 28th
Trip to Texas

Crudder's trip by rail to Kansas City was uneventful. He briefly reflected on the last time he made that trip and being the only passenger of the private rail car his father had built. Smiling to himself, he realized how much more comfortable he was having a coach seat and a simple sleeping compartment.

The stagecoach trip from Kansas City to San Antonio was hot and dusty. It took him two weeks to make that leg of his journey. The time was made that much longer because of the talkative man who was the only other passenger on the stage.

"Did I tell you about the time I was sellin' housewares in the Oklahoma Territory?" asked the man whose name Crudder heard once and quickly forgot. "There weren't many customers in that part of the country. It didn't make me no difference. Some people can't take bein' by themselves. Not me. I'm fine with people or without 'em. Anyway, I was makin' my way across the territory and you know what happened?" Without pausing for John to respond, the boring man plunged on ahead. "Injuns came out of nowhere. Now, I don't have to tell you, I was plenty scared. I mean, I'm a good shot and all, but there were so many of 'em...."

After doing his best to be polite and engage in conversation, John finally realized the only way to get peace and quiet was to either be asleep or feign sleep. Several times, John heard the sometimes drummer say, "You shor do sleep a lot, young feller. I ain't never seen nobody that needed as much sleep as you do."

John smiled inside and was thankful he didn't feel he needed to respond. His thoughts were of Charlotte, the twins, and home. John found with a little practice he was indeed able to sleep while seated on the coach.

✳ ✳ ✳

Arriving in San Antonio at midday, he went to the livery stable and gave a whistle as he walked in. Midnight whinnied in response. John smiled as he walked back to see his great horse pawing the ground and nodding his head up and down.

He could tell Midnight had been freshly groomed. He was pleased the stableman had done as he promised. Crudder had already paid enough to cover all his mount's expenses as well as the extra care he had requested. Regardless, he left the stableman a generous tip for the good care his horse received.

John didn't know if he would stop halfway to Bandera and

camp for the night. It all depended on how much Midnight wanted to run. He knew his mighty horse could easily make it to Bandera by dusk.

He saddled his horse and swung up, wheeling Midnight around to the northwest road out of town. Midnight trotted to the edge of town and waited for a signal from John. He thought he would have some fun with the great steed. Instead of signaling it was fine to run, John kept the reins taut. Midnight shook his head and exhaled an enormous breath that vibrated his lips. John laughed, "All right, boy. I get the message. Let's go home." He gave Midnight his head and the powerful stallion struck out for Bandera.

John let him run for about twenty minutes at a time before reining him in to a gentle lope. He stopped at every stream and pond they passed. Midnight would drink quickly and perk his ears forward ready to hit the road again. It was not long until he recognized his surroundings as being the outer reaches of the H&F Ranch. Home and family were less than an hour away.

Roy Clinton

EPILOGUE

Saturday, September 12th
Bandera, Texas

John realized he had been gone more than two months. Somehow the grass of the H&F seemed lusher than he remembered. The birdsong sounded prettier. Before Slim's house came into view, he had already anticipated his daughters running out to meet him.

It was almost dusk when he rode into the clearing occupied by his home and that of his father-in-law. John let out a whistle and Cora and Claire came running out of the house. "Daddy's home. Daddy's home."

Charlotte came out next followed by her brother, Richie, and Slim. John swung down and grabbed his daughters in each arm. "That's what I've been missing. I love my girls." John planted a kiss on each daughter's cheek.

"I'll take care of Midnight for you, John."

"Thanks, Richie." John let his daughters down but instead of running back to the porch, they each grabbed his legs so he would give them a ride as he made his way to Charlotte.

His wife opened her arms and enveloped him in a hug that lasted longer than John anticipated. Charlotte whispered in his ear. "I'm so glad you're home. I've missed you." He kissed her and expressed his love for her.

Slim came over and slapped John on the back. "We're all glad you're home, son. How'd things go for you?" At that moment, John forgot about his excitement of seeing his family and thought about the emptiness in the Ross home in Philadelphia.

John let go of Charlotte and sat down in one of the rockers on the porch. Charlotte sat beside him and took his hand in hers but remained silent. She felt John wanted to talk but wanted him to be able to wait until he was ready.

"Things didn't go well," he said. "The President commissioned me as his Special Agent and gave me a pardon for past crimes. I didn't feel I had much choice but accept his commission. He wants me to continue being the Midnight Marauder. Then he said he wanted me to be on the Charley Ross case."

Charlotte put her hand to her mouth in shock. "I read about that in the newspaper. How did it turn out?"

"I wasn't able to save the boy. I didn't even get close. I'm not sure I'm cut out for being the Special Agent of the President. In fact, I wrote him a letter from Philadelphia telling him I needed to resign due to my complete failure to accomplish the goal of bringing that little boy home. Charlotte, he was just barely older than the twins. I can't even imagine what I would do if something happened to them."

Charlotte placed her hand on John's leg and squeezed it lightly. She wanted to talk him out of the notion he was a failure but remained silent. John felt the weight of the world on his shoulders. While he knew he couldn't have stopped the murder of Charley Ross, he still felt responsible. Try as he might, he was not able to completely balance the Scales of Justice. Sure, the kidnappers had all paid the ultimate price for their crime. But he still felt a void with the boy's death.

"Before you continue moping around here," said Charlotte, "you need to read this letter. It arrived last week." John noticed the return address was from the President's assistant, Jeffrey Jameson. John couldn't figure out why the President had contacted him again so soon, unless it was to accept his resignation. That must be what it was.

John Crudder
Bandera, Texas

Dear John,

Thank you for your report concerning the kidnapping of Charley Ross. I strongly disagree with your conclusions. While it is true Charley Ross was killed by his kidnappers, I realize in the given circumstances, there was nothing you could have done to have prevented that tragedy.

Thanks to your investigating skills, you were able to track down all those responsible for the kidnapping. The police did not have any clues they could pursue. You found the person who masterminded the kidnapping and, by eliminating him, spared the country a lengthy, painful trial that would likely have encouraged others to copy the crime.

I have received reports from the police departments in Philadelphia and New York City as well as the Pinkerton Agency. All three said they did not have any leads to the kidnapping except what you discovered. Additionally, the three organizations have said you took control of the investigation and coordinated all aspects without marginalizing their efforts.

I was getting ready to send this letter when I received a letter from Christian Ross. He was obviously distraught over the death of his son. But he also said he took comfort in the fact you tracked down each one of the kidnappers and particularly that you found the reason for the kidnapping, the anger of his former partner. He thanked me eloquently for sending you to head up the investigation.

I have also found out you personally paid the cost of the Pinkertons. This is much appreciated since there was no federal money for this expense.

So far as a federal law on kidnapping, I believe the first step is to get the states to enact laws and then for the federal government to support their efforts. I have already been in touch with the governor of Pennsylvania and he assures me he will lead efforts to make kidnapping a felony.

I am certain I have the right man on the job as my Special Agent. Your resignation is not accepted. Take a break. You have earned it. When you have had sufficient rest, I look forward to calling on you again.

Sincerely,
Ulysses S. Grant
President of the United States

John read the letter to himself then folded it as he tried to comprehend what the President had said.

"Well, are you going to tell me what he said?" asked Charlotte.

"Sure. I'm sorry. I was just trying to let his message sink in." John read the letter to Charlotte who smiled proudly at her husband.

"It sounds like you still have a job. I wonder what you'll be called on to do next?"

John gathered her in his arms. "I don't know what the President has in mind. But for now, I think I'll concentrate on lovin' on my wife and my daughters."

John held out his arms and the twins jumped into his lap. "Girls there is something important I need to talk to you about. This is one of the most important things I have ever said to you so I want you to remember it.

"Don't take candy from strangers. If someone you don't know offers you candy, don't take it. Only take candy from Mommy or Daddy or Grandpa or Richie."

The girls looked at each other with confusion. He repeated his words. Then he said they are going to say it together. He said, "Don't take…. Now it's your turn. Don't take what?"

"Candy," said the girls.

"From?" John pressed.

"Strangers!" Both girls threw their hands in the air as they realized they got the words right.

"I'm proud of both of my daughters. Don't take candy from strangers!"

THE END

ACKNOWLEDGMENTS

I would like to say thanks to my wife Kathie, who was the first to read this book and give helpful edits and encouragement throughout the writing process. Thanks for indulging me, especially on the days when I am totally focused on writing to the exclusion of everything else.

I would also like to thank the Top Westerns team: Teresa Lauer publisher who also designs the books and works through hundreds of details to make sure we meet deadlines; Laurie Barboza, who designed the cover; copy editor, Sharon Smith, whose work makes me appear more literate; substantive editor, Maxwell Morelli, whose job it is to make sure the parts fit together properly and to ensure continuity of the series; and finally, R. William James, who produces the audio version of each book. I am also indebted our beta readers, Marc Jankowski, Chris Bryan, Beverley Scobell, Michael Porter, Teresa Lauer, Phil Lauer, and Laurie Barboza. I cannot over estimate the value of this amazing team. Your suggestions helped make this novel better.

If you would like to be a beta reader, get manuscripts before anyone else, and have a chance to shape the final book, please email me at Roy@TopWesterns.com.

As with my other books, I have sought to be historically

accurate in as many details as possible.

When you are in New York City, you might want to look up the restaurant where Douglas and Mosher ate. Today, it is called Old Homestead Steakhouse and it is the oldest continuously operating steakhouse in the United States.

This book is a highly fictionalized account of the Charley Ross kidnapping but it is replete with facts from that case. While John Crudder was not part of the investigation, the Pinkerton Agency was involved. In 1871, just a year after the forming of the Department of Justice, Congress appropriated $50,000 to create a special sub-agency charged with detecting and prosecuting those guilty of violating federal law. The Pinkerton National Detective Agency was contracted to fulfill that role.

During the investigation, every building in Philadelphia was searched. Ultimately, two dozen letters were received from the kidnappers.

The kidnapping was never solved to the satisfaction of the authorities or the family. No clue was discovered as to the motivation for the crime other than to acquire the ransom. Today, when there is a kidnapping, authorities have a well-developed and refined protocol they use to eliminate suspects, beginning with family and acquaintances and then widening the investigation.

There were many mistakes made in this investigation. But to be fair, kidnapping for ransom had never taken place before so the investigators had to learn as they went.

There is no evidence President Grant took any action, though he was sure to know of the kidnapping since it dominated the national news for several months.

The conclusion was changed from historical fact in that the time was compressed to fit the book. And, of course, the Midnight Marauder's involvement is pure fiction. Unfortunately, little Charley Ross was never found. For several decades after the kidnapping, various people came forward claiming to be Charley Ross—presumably to gain access to any inheritance that would have been coming to Charley. There was even one man, Gustave Blair, from Phoenix, who in 1939, succeeded in convincing a judge he was Charley Ross. An interesting addendum to the story is that Mr. Blair, who said he was held in a cave while being kidnapped, spent a great deal of money being declared to be Charley Ross. He said his foster father confessed in 1901 that he was that boy and he had kept quiet all those years because he didn't want to lose him. Blair never made a claim on Charley Ross's inheritance.

The bizarre twist of P.T. Barnum's involvement is presented just the way it happened. Barnum paid Christian Ross ten thousand dollars with the understanding that after Charley was found, he would join the circus. Ross's financial circumstances were so desperate he accepted Barnum's offer, hoping to back out on it after Charley was found by repaying the money he received.

The shootout that resulted in the death of Mosher and Douglas happened pretty much as is presented in this book with the exception that the police were not in attendance. Holmes and Albert Van Brant, along with two gardeners, brought a swift end to the burglars of Justice Van Brant's home, and in doing so, kept the police from learning any more about the kidnapping. Mosher was killed outright but Douglas lived a few minutes more and confessed he and Mosher kidnapped Charley Ross. Douglas said only Mosher knew where the boy was held. He then died before saying anything more.

William Westervelt, who had been fired from the New York City police department for taking bribes, was convicted of complicity in the kidnapping of Charley Ross and served seven years in prison. He was the only one convicted in the kidnapping.

The stranger mentioned at the first of the book is pure conjecture by the author. No such person was ever mentioned in any of the many news reports about the kidnapping.

Christian Ross was heavily in debt and didn't have money to pay the ransom, though at least one wealthy person stepped forward and agreed to pay it. The local authorities encouraged him not to pay for fear it would encourage others to copy the crime.

Just two years after the kidnapping, Ross wrote a best-selling book to raise money for the search for his son. He continued his search for Charley for the rest of his life.

In February 1875, Pennsylvania made kidnapping for extortion a felony crime with serious penalties, the first state to do so. Prior to the Charley Ross case, kidnapping was only a misdemeanor in every state.

It is also interesting to note that the phrase, "Don't take candy from strangers," originated with the Charley Ross kidnapping.

I'm always glad to hear from readers. You may email me at Roy@TopWesterns.com. I make it a point to answer every letter.

Please be patient if it takes me a few days to respond. I may be on a writing retreat or traveling but I will reply.

The next book will be released in a few months. The title is *Purgatory Creek*. You can read a preview on the next few pages. Also, you can listen to all the Top Western books on Audible.com and on iTunes.

Roy Clinton

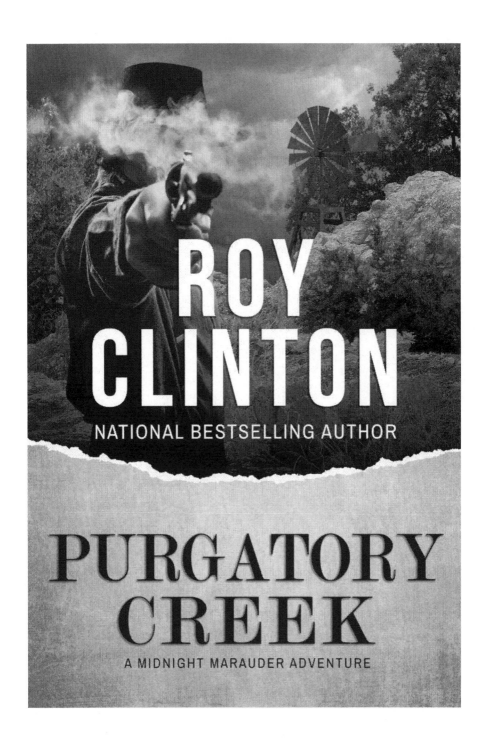

ROY CLINTON

NATIONAL BESTSELLING AUTHOR

PURGATORY CREEK

A MIDNIGHT MARAUDER ADVENTURE

Roy Clinton

PREVIEW OF

PURGATORY CREEK

July, 1874
Huntsville, Texas

The first prisoners arrived at the Huntsville prison in October of 1849. It was quickly dubbed The Walls Unit because a fifteen-foot thick wall surrounded the facility. Oddly, Butch Granger seemed right at home from his first day.

"Hey Butcher," yelled one of the guards. "They say you killed a lot of men before coming here. How many did you kill?"

Granger turned and sneered at the guard. "I killed enough. But I'm not through. You'll be wiping blood off the floor of this prison before I'm done."

The guard pushed the handcuffed man forward causing him to stumble and fall. Granger's hands where cuffed behind his back and attached by chain to his leg irons. Prisoners watched from their cells as the new inmate was being processed. Granger cut his eyes to the guard and let out a sinister laugh. "You can't hurt me none. I'll add you to the list of people I'm gonna kill. In fact, you may be one of the first."

"I'm going to enjoy watching you hang, Butcher."

"Ain't nobody hangin' me. And ain't no prison gonna hold me."

"That's not what I heard," said one of the guards as they hauled Granger to his feet. "They say you were given life in prison so there would be time to try you for the other murders you committed. They'll hang you, all right. And I'll be on the front row smiling when they do it."

Granger hauled back and spit in the guard's face. The guard raised his club and brought it down heavily on Granger's head. Another guard stepped in and began clubbing Granger in the back as he fell to the floor. After several punishing blows, both guards proceeded to use their feet to try to break Granger's ribs and rearrange his face.

The prisoners shouted as they watched the new prisoner being beaten. "Shut up," yelled the first guard as he turned his attention to the cells of the other prisoners. He poked his club through the bars striking several of the men. Then he swung the club hard, hitting the hands of several more men who were holding onto their cell bars. "Let that be a lesson to you. If I hear another peep out of any of you, I'll bring you out here and give you worse than I've given the Butcher."

The prisoners got quiet and looked in horror as they saw the damage the guards had done to Granger's face. Granger was out cold and just lay there bleeding on the concrete floor.

The temperature in the prison was stifling and stayed above ninety degrees throughout the summer. The red brick walls appeared to be sweating but it was just the condensation from breath of the prison population. As if the heat was not bad enough, the smell of urine and feces permeated the atmosphere. Each of the cells had a bucket where the convicts could relieve themselves and defecate. The buckets were only emptied twice a week. The smell was so nauseating that most prisoners habitually breathed through their mouths.

The guards were all dressed alike. They wore dark shirts and matching pants, a cap with a short bill, and a nightstick they used to both intimidate the prisoners and to keep order. But what most prisoners realized was the guards felt they were obligated to dole out punishment to each inmate at every opportunity.

Over the next few weeks, Granger settled into his new surroundings. It was obvious the other convicts feared him. Few would make eye contact with him. He relished his reputation and how quickly his exploits were known throughout the prison population. From the time the first guard called him Butcher, he was never referred to by any other name. Granger enjoyed seeing the fear in the prisoners' eyes and hearing them refer to him as "Mr. Butcher."

During those first several weeks in prison, Granger found

himself in solitary more than once. He didn't mind. It seemed the worse the conditions, the more he liked it. Solitary confinement at the prison was like living in a dungeon. The corridor to the individual cells was so dark the red brick walls looked black. There was one window high on the wall that let in a bit of light but provided very little ventilation. The smell of the slop buckets was nauseating. Guards would often gag when they came into the solitary wing. Granger recalled seeing one of the guards throw up on the metal tray he was carrying to a prisoner. The convict didn't complain when he received his food. Granger figured he probably couldn't see what he was eating.

It was then that Granger grinned to himself as he thought about how he was going to escape from prison. The guard who brought their meals was about the same size as Granger. In the dim light, he thought his resemblance to the guard was remarkable. If he ever got the chance, he thought he could exchange places with the guard and walk out the prison gate.

Granger watched each day for his look-alike to come back into solitary. But the guard never came. A few days later, Granger was taken back to the general population. As he was being led out of solitary, he saw the guard he thought he resembled and realized he was just being rotated back to an assignment in that unit. Granger wasted no time in making sure he was taken back to his isolation cell. He turned to the guard who was escorting him and punched him as hard as he could in the face. As the guard fell, Granger stomped on the guard's hands, one of his favorite ways of inflicting injury. The other nearby guards rushed to Granger and used their clubs to beat him into submission.

Granger was once again knocked unconscious. The guards grabbed his legs and dragged him back to solitary. He was rolled into the cell and the door was locked. As the guards were walking away, Granger came to. He smiled to himself for he had arrived at his preferred destination.

Granger nursed his wounds for several more weeks. The guards no longer delivered his food tray through the slot in his door. Instead, they threw the tray through the slot knowing Granger would then have to gather his food from the floor.

The look-alike guard soon returned to the task of meal delivery. Granger watched him come by each afternoon with the only meal of the day. Granger always stayed away from the cell door so he would not intimidate the guards. He would have loved nothing more than to have seen fear in each guard's face but he had a larger plan which called for him to adopt a gentler manner.

After a few days, the guard delivering his meals stopped throwing the tray through the door slot and set it on the ledge of the slot. Granger called out to the guard. "Thank you."

For the next several days, the guard repeated the behavior as he brought Granger's meal. He would set it on the ledge of the slot and Granger would softly repeat, "Thank you." Granger smiled to himself as he anticipated his next step.

About three weeks after arriving in solitary for his most recent stay, Granger put his plan into motion. When he saw the guard walking toward his cell, he went to the back of the cell, curled into a fetal position and began moaning.

"Get up, Butcher. It's time to eat." Granger just moaned and rocked his body as he pretended to be in great pain.

"Come on, Butcher. Get up. I know there's nothing wrong with you." Granger continued to moan and act as though his pain was excruciating. "If I have to come in there, you're gonna feel the wrath of my nightstick. Get up and come get your food."

Granger continued to moan and gently rock. The guard unlocked the cell door and held his nightstick in his hand. "Come on, Butcher. Get up. I know you're playing possum." He poked Granger in the ribs with the club. It was all Granger could do to keep from flinching as he felt the poke of the nightstick on his bruised ribs. After poking him a second time, the guard leaned down to roll Granger over and see what was wrong with him. As he did, Granger hit him square in the face with his fist. The guard staggered backwards and dropped his nightstick. Granger wasted no time in picking up the club and mercilessly beating the guard in the head. After two blows, Granger knew the guard would not be getting up any time soon. Instead of stopping the brutal assault, Granger continued swinging the club at the guard's head until it looked like an overripe cantaloupe had split open.

Granger removed his clothes and those of the guard. The guard's trousers and shirt fit him perfectly. He put on the guard's shoes, picked up the guard's cap and nightstick, and walked out of the cell, stopping to lock it behind him and set his course for the gate at the end of the corridor. After unlocking it, he walked out of solitary confinement.

Granger walked through the unit and realized no one was

looking at him. Other guards were engaged in conversation. He hoped they wouldn't notice him and would allow him to leave without further incident.

He turned right after leaving solitary, unlocked a door leading to the general prison population, and walked through the unit to the far end. At the end of that cell block, he unlocked another door and turned left toward the main entrance. He bent low as he was passing the main entrance and held his hands to his abdomen.

"Hey, where do you think you're goin'?" shouted one of the guards at the checkpoint.

Granger moaned and kept his head down. "I'm sick. Must have been something I ate. Captain told me to take the rest of the day off." Granger continued walking to the front gate. One of the guards walked up behind him but then kept on walking past him to the front gate.

"I hope you get to feelin' better. And I hope I don't catch what you've got."

"I hope so, too. Sorry to leave you guys shorthanded." With those words, Butch Granger walked out of the Huntsville State Prison and back to freedom. As he walked, he thought about the people he was going to get even with. He was determined to get even with his attorney, the judge, and especially John Crudder. If it had not been for him, he never would have been taken to prison.

END OF PREVIEW

Roy Clinton

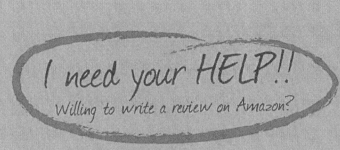

Here's how :
1) go to amazon.com
2) search for Roy Clinton
3) click on appropriate title
4) write a review

The review you write will help get the word
out to others who may benefit.

— Thanks for your help,
Roy Clinton

Made in the USA
San Bernardino, CA
15 June 2020